"I'd like an explanation," Mr. Collins said simply.

Elizabeth raised her eyes. "An explanation? An explanation of what?"

"This!" he said, holding her essay in front of her.

"Well . . ." Elizabeth took a deep breath. "I know it's not the best I could do," she began, "but I was so busy with *The Oracle* last week because everyone was out sick—"

"Elizabeth!" Mr. Collins cut her off. "Please don't make this any harder than it already is. I spent a sleepless night trying to come up with reasons why you would do this, trying to explain it to myself somehow." There was real pain in his eyes when he looked at her. "You're the last person in the world I would have thought would do something like this."

Suddenly Elizabeth realized that she and Mr. Collins weren't talking about the same thing. The anger and disappointment in his face weren't about her essay not being up to her usual standards. It was something else. Something really awful. "Do something like what?" she asked uncertainly.

Bantam Books in the Sweet Valley High series
Ask your bookseller for the books you have missed

SWEET VALLEY High®

ELIZABETH BETRAYED

Written by
Kate William

Created by
FRANCINE PASCAL

BANTAM BOOKS

NEW YORK · TORONTO · LONDON · SYDNEY · AUCKLAND

RL 6, age 12 and up

ELIZABETH BETRAYED
A Bantam Book / November 1992

Sweet Valley High is a registered trademark of Francine Pascal
Conceived by Francine Pascal
Produced by Daniel Weiss Associates, Inc.
33 West 17th Street
New York, NY 10011
Cover art by James Mathewuse

ISBN 0-553-29235-8

Published simultaneously in the United States and Canada

Bantam Books are published by Bantam Books, a division of Bantam Doubleday Dell Publishing Group, Inc. Its trademark, consisting of the words "Bantam Books" and the portrayal of a rooster, is Registered in U.S. Patent and Trademark Office and in other countries. Marca Registrada. Bantam Books, 666 Fifth Avenue, New York, New York 10103.

PRINTED IN THE UNITED STATES OF AMERICA

OPM   0 9 8 7 6 5 4 3 2 1

ELIZABETH
BETRAYED

One

"I know you appreciate good writing. You even write a little yourself," Rod Sullivan was saying to his girlfriend, Olivia Davidson, as they drove to Sweet Valley High on Monday morning. "Don't you agree with me that Elizabeth Wakefield has a really special talent?"

Olivia fiddled with the strap of her bag, looking straight ahead of her. Usually she loved driving to school with Rod. It was one of the few times all day when they could actually be alone together. This morning, however, she felt as though there were three of them in the car: Olivia, Rod, and Elizabeth Wakefield. Rod hadn't stopped talking about Elizabeth since Olivia got in.

Rod nudged her. "Hey, sleepyhead! Didn't you hear me? Don't you think Elizabeth has a special talent?"

Olivia forced herself to smile back at him. She, Rod, and Elizabeth were all on the staff of *The Oracle*, Sweet Valley High's school newspaper, but it was Elizabeth who was the star reporter. Lately Elizabeth seemed to be Rod's favorite topic of conversation. When, a few days earlier, Olivia had suggested that his admiration of her was going a little far, Rod had assured her that his interest in Elizabeth was only that of a friend. Even so, she wished he would find something else to be so enthusiastic about.

"Of course. I think Elizabeth's amazing," she said, trying to sound enthusiastic herself. "Everyone knows she's a terrific writer. Where would the paper be without her?"

Rod shook his head. "I bet you that twenty years from now she'll win the Pulitzer Prize for journalism, and we'll be telling all our friends that we used to know her when."

Olivia smiled grimly. Not only did Olivia work on *The Oracle*, but she also edited *Visions*, the school literary magazine, almost single-handedly, and she was a very talented painter as well. But she couldn't remember Rod ever suggesting that *she* would win something someday. "I'm sure you're right," she said flatly.

"Of course I'm right." He shook his head. "Didn't you love that piece she did for the *L.A. Times*?" Rod apparently couldn't get over the fact that someone they went to school with had had work published in a paper like the *Times*.

Olivia looked at him. "I didn't get a chance to read it. I guess I was just too busy trying to get

2

some new ideas together for the next issue of *Visions*," she explained. Finally seeing a break in the Elizabeth Wakefield monologue, she went on quickly, "In fact, I was hoping to discuss some of my ideas with you."

"Me?" Rod looked surprised. "I know the magazine means a lot to you, Liv, but I already told you I'm not going to have any extra time for it."

Olivia knew. How could she not know? Rod, who was a gifted graphic artist, had given her some invaluable help with *Visions* when she first began it, but he had made it clear that he was too busy with his work for *The Oracle* and his own projects to become really involved. Olivia also knew that he wasn't all that interested in *Visions*. "I know, it's not nearly as important as *The Oracle*," she replied a little bitterly. She could feel her cheeks burning.

Rod reached over and took her hand. "It's not that I'm putting *Visions* down or anything," he said gently. "You do a great job on the magazine. It's just that stories and poetry and stuff like that don't seem as real to me as news articles."

Olivia watched the houses go by. What was the use of trying to explain to him again that "stories and poetry and stuff like that" were every bit as *real* as news articles? At least to her they were.

Rod steered the red Honda into the high school parking lot and pulled into a space. "Don't forget to read that article of Elizabeth's," he said as he turned off the engine. "It's really good." He smiled. "It might even inspire you."

Olivia didn't smile back. She was not a petty or jealous person by nature, but she was getting pretty

3

sick and tired of hearing Rod constantly talk about how intelligent and talented Elizabeth was. She unfastened her seat belt and got out of the car. "Thanks for the advice," she said, slamming the door shut. "I just hope the *L.A. Times* doesn't offer Elizabeth a job before we graduate. Without her around to inspire me, I'd probably never put out another issue of the magazine again."

Rod got out, too, falling into step beside her. He put his arm around her shoulders. "Hey," he said, "do I detect a little jealousy here?"

"Jealousy?" Olivia didn't meet his eyes. "Don't be ridiculous. Of course I'm not jealous."

He leaned his head close to hers. "I just think Elizabeth's a good journalist," he said softly. "You're the girl I'm crazy about."

She turned to look at Rod. His eyes were looking right into hers. Olivia smiled her first real smile of the day.

Elizabeth Wakefield walked across the school parking lot with her identical twin sister, Jessica, who was chatting happily about the beach party she had been to the day before.

"You really should have come," Jessica said with her usual bubbly enthusiasm. "On a scale of one to ten it was a definite twelve."

Elizabeth smiled. Nothing with Jessica was ever simply good or bad. It was either fantastic or completely awful. "I'm sure it was great," she said, "but I just had too much to do."

Jessica frowned in mock seriousness. "If you ask me, Elizabeth Wakefield, your problem is that you

4

work too hard. Life's for living, not typing." She shook her head. "You're the only person I know who would rather spend the weekend in her room with her word processor than at the beach with her friends." She grinned impishly. "I'm so glad I only *look* like you."

Elizabeth grinned back. Jessica was right. Even though the two girls looked exactly the same, from their sun-streaked blond hair to their blue-green eyes and the tiny dimple in their left cheeks, underneath they were as different as spring and fall. Jessica was fun-loving and frivolous. Her three favorite things were parties, shopping, and boys. Elizabeth, however, was quieter and more serious. She preferred spending time with her best friend, Enid Rollins, and her boyfriend, Todd Wilkins, to having a busy social life.

"I have to work hard on my articles for *The Oracle* if I'm ever going to be a professional writer," she said. "And besides, I'm having a tough time getting started on my English essay for Mr. Collins."

"I never worry about that sort of thing," Jessica said airily.

Elizabeth decided not to point out that Jessica rarely worried about much of anything. Seeing Olivia Davidson and Rod Sullivan up ahead of them, she decided to change the subject. "Doesn't Olivia look great today?" she asked, giving her sister a nudge. "She really has a terrific sense of style."

Jessica nodded. "She's a little too artsy for me, but she's still cool." Her eyes sparkled mischievously. "Even if she *is* as intense as you are."

5

"Maybe that's why we like each other so much," Elizabeth answered. "Because we have so much in common." She touched her twin's shoulder. "I think I'll go catch up with her. See you later."

Elizabeth had just reached Olivia and Rod inside the school entrance when Penny Ayala, editor-in-chief of *The Oracle*, came racing down the hallway toward them.

"Elizabeth! Olivia! Rod!" she shouted. Her face was bright with color and her hazel eyes shone.

Elizabeth couldn't remember ever seeing Penny so excited before. "What is it?" she called back.

"You're not going to believe this," Penny said as she screeched to a stop next to them. "You're just not going to believe it!" She looked from one to another, unable to stop smiling. "I've been chosen for the Washington Correspondent Program!" she announced in a rush. "Isn't that terrific? Out of all the thousands of high school editors in the country, they picked me!"

"That's wonderful!" Elizabeth threw her arms around her friend. She knew how much this meant to Penny. The Washington Correspondent Program gave a few of the top high school editors the opportunity to spend two weeks in Washington, D.C., following a senator around, just as an actual reporter would.

Olivia hugged Penny, too. "Congratulations," she said. "No one deserves this more than you."

"That's right," Elizabeth said. "You're the best high school editor in the country. Who else would they pick?" She looked to Rod and Olivia for agree-

6

ment. Olivia was nodding her head, but Rod wasn't looking at Penny. He was smiling at Elizabeth.

Rod suddenly turned back to the others. "We'll have to go somewhere after school to celebrate," he said.

Penny laughed. "I don't know if I have time to celebrate. I leave on Friday, and I have about a million things to do before I go."

Rod put one arm around Penny's shoulders. "We won't take no for an answer," he told her. "Will we?"

Elizabeth smiled. "Of course not." She turned to Penny. "Even William Randolph Hearst must have stopped for a double-cheese pizza now and then."

Todd raised his juice container. "To Elizabeth Wakefield! Acting editor-in-chief of *The Oracle.*"

Enid raised her carton of milk. "Here, here!"

Elizabeth blushed. "Come on, you two," she said. "Penny heard only this morning that she's going to Washington. I'm sure she hasn't had time even to think about asking someone to stand in for her."

Enid picked up her sandwich. "But she will have to ask someone, won't she?" she reasoned. "She can't leave the paper without an editor for two whole weeks."

Elizabeth nodded. Once she had gotten over the surprise of Penny's news, she'd remembered that very thing: that Penny would have to appoint someone to act as editor-in-chief while she was away. Someone who was responsible. Someone who was dedicated. *Someone like me!* Elizabeth had thought, her heart skipping a beat.

"But that doesn't mean she'll choose me," she protested now. "There are a lot of hard-working, talented people on the paper, you know."

Todd made a face. "Don't be so modest, Liz," he said. "You know as well as we do that you're the obvious choice."

Elizabeth blushed again. Deep down, she secretly thought that she was the obvious choice—or at least one of the obvious choices—but she wanted the job so much that she was afraid to be too confident about getting it.

"That's right," Enid agreed. "No one works harder than you do."

"And no one else has already filled in as editor like you did when Penny was out sick," Todd reminded her.

"And no one else has been published by the *L.A. Times,*" Enid added.

Elizabeth pushed her plate away. She was much too excited and nervous even to pretend to eat. "But what about Olivia?" she asked. In Elizabeth's opinion, Olivia was the only other obvious choice. She didn't have as much journalistic experience as Elizabeth, but she had enormous editorial ability and flair—and Penny knew it.

Todd's expression became grimly serious. "Olivia?" he asked. "Olivia Davidson?" He slapped his forehead. "I forgot about her. Maybe you *are* in trouble, Liz."

Elizabeth tried not to look disappointed. She had

been expecting Todd to tell her that she didn't have to worry about Olivia.

Enid punched Todd in the arm. "Stop teasing her," she ordered. "Can't you see she's really nervous about this?"

Todd broke into a huge grin, leaned over, and put his arm around Elizabeth. "Lucky for you Olivia already has too much to do with *Visions.*"

Elizabeth smiled. Todd was right. Penny probably wouldn't choose Olivia because she was doing too much already. *Lucky for me is right,* she thought.

"Two weeks is a long time," Rod said as he set down his tray. "She'll have to appoint someone. Now, I wonder who that someone could be?" he added in a teasing tone of voice.

Olivia slipped into the chair across from him. She knew that Rod meant Elizabeth. And to be fair, Elizabeth had been the first person Olivia had thought of, too. But then someone else had occurred to Olivia. Someone who had a vast amount of editorial experience. Someone who was a talented writer and a tireless worker.

Olivia looked at Rod as he lifted a forkful of pasta salad to his mouth. "Well, actually," she said evenly, "I was thinking Penny might ask me."

"You?"

Olivia glared at him. "Yes, *me,*" she said coolly. "What's so outrageous about that?"

Rod shook his head. "There's nothing outrageous about it, Liv. It's just that you're already editing

Visions. And, good as you are, journalism's not really your specialty. Besides, Elizabeth is already Penny's right-hand person."

Olivia felt her confidence slipping away. Rod was probably right. Why would Penny ask her when Elizabeth was available? Elizabeth had more experience, she had worked closely with Penny for ages, and she already did a lot of the editorial work anyway. She wasn't just the obvious choice, she was the only choice.

"I didn't mean actually ask me to run the paper," she said quickly. "I just thought she might ask me to help Elizabeth out. I do know a lot about editing and layout, you know."

Rod picked up his fork again. "Yeah, but you're much more knowledgeable about fiction and poetry, and it seems like *Visions* keeps you pretty busy."

Olivia's confidence ebbed a little more. She thought about the things Penny and Elizabeth had said about *Visions.* That it was well done. That it showed imagination. That it must be nice to work on something that didn't come out every week, because she really had time to give it her all. She had thought they were complimenting her, but now she wondered. Maybe they had really been saying, "Go away now, Olivia, we have something important to work on. Something real."

She shoved her plate away, too depressed to eat. "Maybe you're right," she said in a soft, defeated voice.

Jessica was humming to herself as she got her things out of her locker. She had survived another Monday, school was over, and she was going home.

"Jessica!" called a voice nearby. "Jessica!"

Jessica turned around. Coming down the hallway toward her was Annie Whitman, one of her fellow cheerleaders. Jessica smiled happily. "Hi, Annie!"

But Annie, Jessica suddenly realized, did not seem to be in a happy mood.

"I want to talk to you, Jessica Wakefield," Annie whispered angrily. She glanced around her to make sure there was no one else listening.

The smile died on Jessica's lips. "What is it?" she asked, genuinely puzzled.

"What is it?" Annie repeated sarcastically. "Are you going to stand there and tell me that you don't know what it is?"

Jessica shut her locker and backed off a few steps. Sweet Valley High cheerleaders didn't usually go around slugging one another, but from the look in Annie's eyes it occurred to Jessica that there might be a first time. "Yes," she said as calmly as she could. "I have no idea why you're so upset."

"Well, let me give you a hint, then." Annie folded her arms across her chest. "Tony."

"Tony?" Jessica blinked, still confused. Tony Esteban was Annie's boyfriend. "What about Tony?"

"Don't pretend with me, Judas Wakefield," Annie snarled. "I know you know that he's been seeing another girl. You knew, and you didn't tell me! I'm supposed to be your friend, but you didn't tell me he was running around with someone else, making a fool out of me!"

11

Jessica felt the color drain from her face. It was true. She *had* seen Tony at least half a dozen times with someone else, but she'd never considered telling Annie.

Annie pointed to Jessica. "You did know! Tony told me you did. He said he thought I knew, since you knew. He thought you'd told me and that I didn't mind."

Jessica regained her composure. "Calm down, will you, Annie?" She tried to reach for Annie's hand, but Annie pulled away roughly. "First of all," Jessica said, trying to sound as reasonable and calm as she could, "I didn't *know*. I saw him with some girl a couple of times, but it could have been completely innocent. It could have—"

Tears were streaming down Annie's cheeks. "You let me go on thinking everything was fine." She wiped her eyes with the sleeve of her sweater. "I bet you told everyone else, though. The whole school's probably been laughing at me."

Jessica was indignant. The only person she had mentioned it to was her best friend, Lila Fowler, and Lila had been sworn to secrecy. "That's not true! I *am* your friend, Annie. I just didn't want to upset you."

"Well, thanks very much," Annie said coldly. "Thanks for sparing my feelings. But in the future you don't have to worry about what you do or don't tell me, Jessica Wakefield, because I'm never speaking to you again so long as I live!"

Elizabeth climbed into the Jeep and fastened her seat belt. "Isn't it great about Penny?" she said. "I really envy her. It's just about the best thing that could have happened."

Jessica showed less enthusiasm than she would have if she had just been told Penny had bought a new silk shirt. "Personally, I'd rather have a ring through my nose," she said sourly.

Elizabeth started the engine and gave her twin a look. "You could be a little nicer about it, you know. Maybe it isn't what you'd want to do, but it happens to be really important to Penny."

"Oh, I know," Jessica said with a sigh. "I didn't mean to sound so nasty. It's just that I had this big fight with Annie Whitman today and it's put me in a really bad mood."

Elizabeth pulled the Jeep out of the parking lot and into traffic. "With Annie? What about? I thought you two were good friends."

"*Were* is the right word." Jessica made a face. "She says she'll never speak to me again." As they headed toward home Jessica told Elizabeth about the scene she had had with Annie. "It was just awful," she finished. "You'd think the whole thing was my fault, the way she described it."

"It does sound like maybe she overreacted," Elizabeth said carefully. "But if you think about it, Jess, she does have a point. Friends should tell each other things like that. I mean, what are friends for?"

Jessica moaned. "But it's *because* she's my friend that I didn't say anything. I know what happens when you tell people things they don't want to hear. They get upset, and then the next thing you know, they're mad at you."

"Annie couldn't be much madder at you than she is right now," Elizabeth pointed out. "The truth is the truth. You can't go wrong by telling the truth." She glanced at her twin. "After all, honesty *is* the best policy."

Two

Olivia hadn't taken two steps past the doorway of Sweet Valley High on Tuesday morning when Jennifer Mitchell, another writer for *The Oracle*, rushed up to her. "Have you heard?" she asked excitedly. "Penny's appointed Elizabeth editor-in-chief while she's in Washington!"

Olivia couldn't respond at first. Jennifer's words echoed in her head: *Penny's appointed Elizabeth editor-in-chief.* Finally, realizing that Jennifer was waiting for her to say something, Olivia swallowed the lump that had formed in her throat and managed a smile. "That's great," she said, hoping she sounded more enthusiastic than she felt. "That means it'll be business as usual."

Why are you so surprised? Olivia asked herself after Jennifer was gone. *Rod was right. You knew it was going to be Elizabeth; there was never any contest.*

Olivia had covered a few more feet in the direction of her locker when John Pfeifer, *The Oracle*'s sports editor and Jennifer Mitchell's boyfriend, called to her. "Did you hear about Elizabeth?" he shouted.

Olivia decided not to pretend that she didn't know what he was talking about. She nodded, forcing the smile back to her face. "Yes," she said. "It's terrific." And then, afraid she might cry, she bolted away from him, in exactly the direction she didn't want to be going.

Olivia took deep breaths and tried to calm herself down as she hurried along. *Stop it*, she ordered. *You're acting like a little kid. You know that if you were Penny, you would have chosen Elizabeth, too. And besides, Elizabeth is your friend. You should be happy for her.*

By the time Olivia finally reached her locker, she was feeling better. She was going to try to be happy for Elizabeth, she really was. When she saw Elizabeth, she would congratulate her warmly and sincerely.

"There you are," said a voice right behind her. Olivia turned around. It was Rod. "I've been looking for you everywhere. Have you heard about Elizabeth?"

Olivia nodded.

He leaned against the lockers while she got out her books. "It's about time Elizabeth had a chance to show what she can really do," he said.

Olivia threw her jacket into her locker and slammed it shut. *I wonder when I'm going to have a chance to show what I can do*, she asked herself.

16

* * *

"You've got to help me, Liz," Jessica said as she burst into the kitchen on Wednesday morning. "I'm counting on you."

Elizabeth looked up from the book she was reading. "I don't like the sound of that," she said with a laugh. "Every time you say you need my help, I wind up in trouble."

Jessica dropped into her chair and gave her sister an exasperated look. She was perfectly willing to admit that once or twice some idea of hers had gotten Elizabeth into a tiny little scrape, but her twin always acted as though trouble were Jessica's middle name. Jessica waved the cereal box at Elizabeth. "It's nothing like that. I just need you to help me come up with some excuse for not going to the dirt bike race with Sam on Saturday." Sam Woodruff, Jessica's boyfriend, was a serious dirt bike racer. This meant that Jessica was a serious dirt bike race spectator, whether she liked it or not.

Mrs. Wakefield looked over her coffee cup at Jessica, but didn't say anything.

"Me?" Elizabeth started laughing. "Why me? You're the one with all the schemes and plans."

Jessica nibbled on a cornflake. "Yeah, but you're the creative one. You're the writer." She gazed musingly at her spoon. "I need something simple but original."

"You mean something he hasn't heard before."

Jessica ignored her. "Something totally convincing."

"Forget it," Elizabeth said. She held up the book in her hands. "I need to hold on to all the creative

17

ability I have if I'm ever going to understand the use of visual imagery in literature and painting enough to be able to write an essay on it."

Mrs. Wakefield put down her cup with a clatter. "Might I be so bold as to ask the real reason you don't want to go watch Sam race?" she asked Jessica.

Jessica shrugged. "Sure. I'm tired of standing up to my ankles in mud all by myself while he rides around having a good time all afternoon."

"And Lila wants you to go shopping with her," Elizabeth guessed.

Jessica glared at her. Sometimes it was very difficult having a twin. A twin wasn't like a regular sister. A twin could practically read your mind. At least hers could.

"Why don't you just tell Sam the truth?" Mrs. Wakefield asked. "I'm sure he'd understand."

"Tell him the truth?" Jessica rolled her eyes. "Mom, I can't tell him the truth. What kind of person do you think I am? I don't want to hurt his feelings. He thinks I love watching him race."

Elizabeth smirked. "I wonder where he got that idea from."

"Well, of course he got it from me," Jessica said. "I'm not going to tell my boyfriend that his favorite activity in the world puts me to sleep faster than watching a movie with subtitles. What if he finds someone who likes it as much as he does? Then where will I be?"

Mrs. Wakefield picked up her coffee cup again. "Well, you're not being very honest with him, that's for sure," she said. "And you don't build a strong

18

relationship on excuses. You build it on truthfulness and trust."

Jessica groaned. "You're way behind the times, Mom. These days, excuses work just fine."

Ever since Penny had asked Elizabeth to stand in for her at the paper, Elizabeth hadn't been able to think of much else. Editor-in-chief! Even though she had taken over for Penny once before when Penny was out sick, this time seemed different and more important. No matter how hard she tried, she couldn't stop fantasizing about it. It filled her mind as she got ready for school in the morning and while she did her homework in the evening. While she ate, she pictured herself winning a special award for her first issue. She pretended she was being asked to join the staff of the *L.A. Times* while she got ready for bed.

And at that moment, as she walked to class with Todd, she was daydreaming about being asked to take on the editorship of *The Oracle* permanently because Penny had decided to stay in Washington.

"Elizabeth." Todd gave her a shake. "Elizabeth, did you hear me? I can have lunch with you today after all. I promised Hal Sylvester I'd help him study for our math test, but he and our teacher are both out with the flu."

Elizabeth brought herself back to reality with an effort. She turned to him with a puzzled expression. "Flu? Who has the flu?"

Todd shook his head. "Earth to Elizabeth Wakefield," he teased. "Are you the only person in this school who doesn't know that the flu's going around? Haven't you noticed that your classes are a little emptier today than they were yesterday?"

Elizabeth frowned. She had been paying so little attention to everything for the last day or so that she probably wouldn't have noticed if her classes were completely empty. "Of course I've noticed," she fibbed. "I'm a trained journalist. I don't miss anything."

They stopped in front of her English class, and Todd gave her a quick kiss. "Just make sure you don't miss anything Mr. Collins tells you," Todd warned her with a grin. "Quarter grade reports are coming up."

"Don't worry," Elizabeth promised. "I'm having so much trouble with this essay he assigned that I may memorize every word he says."

But only minutes after Mr. Collins began his lecture, Elizabeth had forgotten what she had said to Todd. While Mr. Collins talked about symbols and imagination, she found herself doing some imagining of her own. She imagined it was Wednesday, the afternoon the paper was put together and delivered to the printer. Mr. Collins, *The Oracle*'s faculty adviser, was going through the final layout with her. *Elizabeth*, he was saying in her mind, *I can hardly believe what a perfect and professional job you've done. You're obviously a natural.*

It wasn't until the bell rang that Elizabeth managed to tear herself away from her fantasy. She looked around. Her classmates were already leaving the room.

"Don't forget," Mr. Collins was saying. "Your essays are due a week from Tuesday. No excuses."

Rod Sullivan, who sat behind Elizabeth, leaned forward. "It's a good thing he gave us this lecture today," he said, "or I wouldn't have a clue what to do for my essay."

Elizabeth shook her head. "Me neither," she said.

"So here's my idea," Olivia said. She couldn't keep the excitement out of her voice. "I'm going to do a special issue of *Visions* on the environment." She looked from Elizabeth to Penny to Todd. She wasn't sure whether they seemed interested or puzzled. "You know," she explained. "All the poems and stories and artwork will be about the earth and its problems." She unwrapped her straw. "It seems to me that a literary magazine can be just as relevant as a newspaper. The point is to make people aware."

"That's brilliant, Olivia!" Elizabeth exclaimed. "What a great idea!"

"That *is* a great idea," Todd agreed. "I wish I had some artistic or literary talent. I'd love to do something to help the rain forests."

Penny nodded her head. "It sounds wonderful. I wish I'd thought of it, that's for sure." She made a sympathetic face. "But I don't envy you the work you're letting yourself in for, Olivia. At least I have a staff to rely on for the paper. All you have is yourself. How are you going to get people to contribute?"

Olivia smiled. "To tell you the truth, I've been working on that for days." She reached into her backpack and pulled out a cylinder of paper. "Here's the rough of the poster I finally came up

21

with." She pushed her lunch aside and began to unroll the artwork. It had taken her four days to complete it, but she was proud of the results. In the center of the poster she had sketched a view of the earth from space. Above it she had printed in bold black letters: "The Planet Earth. Where Do You Stand on It?" Below the illustration were details of the issue and where contributors could send their work.

Elizabeth pushed a strand of hair back from her face. "It looks fantastic." She looked at Olivia with open admiration. "How did you manage to do this so quickly?"

"Oh, there was nothing to it," Olivia said, laughing. "I just didn't do anything else all week."

It was true. From the moment on Monday afternoon when the idea for an environmental issue first came to her, Olivia's mind had been completely occupied with it. She had decided that she was going to show everyone exactly what she could do, not by sulking over her disappointment at not being asked to help with *The Oracle* while Penny was away, but by producing an issue of *Visions* that would make everyone stand up and take notice. Not only was she genuinely excited about her work, but those unpleasant feelings of jealousy and resentment that she had begun to feel toward Elizabeth had vanished completely.

Todd gave Olivia a thumbs-up sign. "If there's anything I can do to help out, just tell me," he said. "I may not be able to write or draw, but I can type with two fingers, and I can cut and paste."

Elizabeth bit her lip, looking thoughtful. "You

know," she said slowly, "I may have a few poems that are right for this." She smiled shyly at Olivia. "I've really only just started writing poetry, but if you'd like to take a look . . ."

Olivia was feeling so good about her project that she didn't have to pretend to be delighted by Elizabeth's offer. A contribution from Elizabeth would be wonderful, and it would probably encourage others. "Really? That would be great. When can I see them?"

Elizabeth turned pink. "I wouldn't want you to think that I carry my poetry around with me everywhere I go," she said with a nervous laugh. "But it just so happens that the poems I'm thinking of are in my desk in the *Oracle* office."

This is a sign that this project is really going to work, Olivia thought happily. "In that case, why don't you bring them to my house after school this afternoon? I'll read them right away."

Elizabeth picked up her sandwich. "I'll be there," she said. She nodded toward Penny. "I have to have a meeting with our Washington correspondent first, but I'll come straight over after that."

A few days earlier, if Elizabeth had told Olivia that she had to have a meeting with Penny about the newspaper, it would have made Olivia's heart sink. But not anymore. She was determined to produce the best magazine Sweet Valley High had ever seen, and that was all that mattered. Olivia began to reroll the poster. "Great," she said. "I'll be waiting."

Penny checked off the last thing on her list. "Well, I guess we've covered everything," she said.

Elizabeth looked at the notes she had taken. Even though she had acted as editor-in-chief once before, and even though she knew how the paper worked as well as Penny herself did, seeing everything she had to do written down like that made her feel a little panicky.

Penny leaned over and touched her arm. "Don't look so worried." She laughed. "I know you can handle it. You'll be fine."

Elizabeth tried to look as confident as Penny sounded. She had been going around in a dream, imagining everyone praising her for her amazing editorial ability, but the reality was that she was taking on an enormous job. "I hope you're right," she said. "But somehow, the thought of having all this responsibility without you around . . ." Elizabeth made a face. "It's a little like performing on a trapeze without a net."

"But you do have a net," Penny said. "If you run into any trouble, just ask Olivia for help."

A warm rush of relief spread over Elizabeth. *Olivia! Of course!*

"I thought of asking her to give you a hand myself," Penny was saying, "but she has so much to do as it is that I didn't want to put any extra pressure on her. You know how conscientious she is. People are always dumping things on her because they know she'll do them, and do them well."

Elizabeth rolled her eyes. "Tell me about it," she said. "With all the work she does on *Visions*, sometimes I think she makes me look lazy."

Penny shook her head in admiration. "I really

24

don't know how she does it. It's hard enough coming up with ideas for the paper."

Elizabeth picked up her books. "I bet Olivia's going to be really famous someday," she said. She tossed back her hair. "And you and I are going to tell everyone that we knew her when."

Elizabeth sat at the Davidsons' kitchen table, watching Olivia read through her poems. She had been there for over an hour already, but they had so much to talk about that the time had gone by quickly. *I really should try to spend more time with Olivia*, Elizabeth said to herself. *She's not only intelligent, but also one of the most interesting people I know.*

"These are really good," Olivia said at last. "Especially for a beginner." She held up two of the poems. "I won't be able to tell if these are absolutely right for this issue until I've got more material together, but if you don't mind, I'd like to hold on to them."

"Mind? I'm thrilled!"

"And of course, if you want to write some more in the meantime . . ."

"Don't encourage me," Elizabeth said. "Now that I've started, I'm always writing poems. I don't know why, but I enjoy it almost more than anything."

"Really?" Olivia looked suddenly shy. "Me, too."

"You?" Elizabeth tried to hide her surprise. Olivia was *The Oracle*'s arts editor, she ran *Visions*, and she was Sweet Valley High's most talented painter. Elizabeth couldn't help wondering how she found the time to write poetry as well.

Olivia shrugged. "I don't usually tell anyone, if you want to know the truth. But sometimes I just have to stop whatever else I'm doing because an idea comes to me out of the blue." She laughed. "Don't you remember that time I got into trouble in gym because I just walked off the volleyball court?"

Elizabeth grinned. "We had a twenty-minute lecture on sportsmanship and team spirit because of you."

Olivia shook her head wryly. "I know it sounds insane, but I was suddenly overcome by an idea for a poem about motion."

Elizabeth laughed. "And all this time I thought you were just a terrific artist!"

"Painting's my first passion, but I love poetry, too." Olivia said, looking down, shyly.

Why should anyone feel embarrassed about writing poems? Elizabeth wondered. Especially someone like Olivia. Knowing how intense she was, and what a perfectionist, Elizabeth guessed that her work was probably very good.

"I don't understand, though," Elizabeth said. "Why don't you want to tell anyone?"

Olivia shrugged. "I'm not really sure. I guess it's because I used to write a lot of poems when I was little and everyone at school always teased me about them. You know what kids are like. And now . . . well, most people don't take poetry very seriously." She laughed. "Even Rod. I think he thinks poetry is all about daffodils and things like that."

"I know what you mean," Elizabeth said. She made a face. "I live with Jessica Wakefield, remem-

26

ber. She'd rather read the back of a cereal box than a poem."

Olivia looked down at her hands and cleared her throat. "I don't suppose you—I mean, if you have a few minutes . . . I don't want you to think that you *have* to . . . "

Elizabeth couldn't help laughing. "Olivia, are you trying to ask me if I'd read some of your poems?"

Relief spread across Olivia's pretty face. "Would you?"

It was incredible to Elizabeth that someone who exuded confidence and originality the way Olivia did could be so insecure about something that was obviously important to her. Elizabeth smiled. "It would be an honor."

I must be crazy, Olivia thought to herself as she put another piece of paper into her typewriter. Not only had Elizabeth said she thought Olivia's poems were exceptionally good, but she'd also convinced Olivia to submit some of them to the arts section of *The Sweet Valley News*. Olivia had protested that the arts editor wasn't going to publish poems by some unknown high school student.

"You may be an unknown high school student," Elizabeth had told her, "but you're also a first-rate poet. Why don't you let the editor decide whether they should be printed or not?"

So, Thursday night, Olivia was typing up her three best poems and feeling happier than she had in a long time. Even if the poems were turned down, it felt good to try.

27

Olivia had just begun typing the third poem when the telephone rang.

"You sound like you're in a good mood," Rod said when she answered.

"I'm in a great mood," Olivia said. "Elizabeth came over this afternoon, and we—"

"Elizabeth? I didn't know you were having Elizabeth over."

"It was sort of on the spur of the moment," Olivia said, anxious to tell him how positive Elizabeth had been about her writing. "We were talking so much that she even stayed for supper. She read—"

"Gee," Rod interrupted, "I wish I'd known. It would have been fun to hang out with you two. Didn't you have a good time with her and Todd and Penny the other day, when we went out to celebrate Penny's winning the job in Washington?"

"Well, yes," said Olivia. "I had a great time. But I don't see what that has to do with this afternoon." The truth was that it hadn't occurred to her to ask Rod over. She had wanted to talk to Elizabeth about poetry, and Olivia knew that Rod had about as much interest in talking about poetry as he had in talking about tadpoles. "Anyway," she said, "I thought you said you had to work on your art project this afternoon."

"I could have taken a break for an hour," Rod said. "Hey, you know what we should do sometime?" he went on. "We should double-date with Elizabeth and Todd. Wouldn't that be fun?"

Olivia gave up. When Rod didn't want to discuss

28

something, there was no use in fighting it. "Sure," she said. "That's a great idea."

"I can't believe this," Jessica wailed into the phone. "I was really looking forward to the race tomorrow, but now my mother's making me go shopping with her."

Sam laughed. "I've never heard you complain about going shopping before."

"This is different," Jessica said, trying to sound despondent. "She wants me to help her pick out a special anniversary present for my grandparents." Although not strictly the truth, this was so close to the truth that it was almost the same thing. Her parents *were* going shopping on Saturday to buy a present for her grandparents, and Lila *was* insisting that Jessica go shopping with her.

"Well, I can understand if she needs you . . ." Sam said, clearly trying to hide his disappointment. "But are you sure you can't talk her out of it? You know you always bring me luck."

Jessica sighed dramatically as Elizabeth came into the room. "I've tried, Sam," she said, sounding heartbroken and very sincere. "But she won't budge. You know how she gets. She thinks it's the responsible thing to do."

Sam laughed again. "What, you not responsible? I can't believe my ears."

"Very funny," Jessica said. "I'm glad you can laugh, Sam Woodruff. You're going to be having a good time tomorrow while I look at boring vases."

When she hung up, Jessica found herself face to

face with Elizabeth, who was standing at the foot of the bed, frowning.

"Don't start with me," Jessica said quickly.

Elizabeth put her hands on her hips. "What do you mean, don't start with you? I really can't believe you, Jess! You're going to get caught lying in the end. Why don't you just tell Sam the truth?"

There were times when Jessica couldn't help wondering why everyone thought Elizabeth was so smart. "Really, Liz, you don't know much about guys, do you?" She gave her sister a pitying look. "If I told Sam the real reason, he'd wind up sulking all Saturday night. This way we'll have a great time *and* I won't have to spend the afternoon up to my knees in mud."

Elizabeth shook her head. "You know what they say: `Oh, what a tangled web we weave, when first we practice to deceive!' "

"You know what else they say?" Jessica snapped back.

Her sister eyed her quizzically.

"What you don't know can't hurt you!"

Three

"Maybe we should get your parents something really different this year," Mrs. Wakefield said to Mr. Wakefield. "Something they would never buy for themselves in a million years."

Ned Wakefield didn't look up from his paper. "That sounds fine to me, dear."

Elizabeth gave her mother a sympathetic look. She was glad that she wasn't going shopping with her father.

Just then there was the sound of a car pulling into the driveway and then the slam of a door. Jessica downed her juice in one gulp. "There's Lila," she said. "Come on in!" she shouted as Lila appeared at the back door. "I'll be ready in a minute."

Lila stepped into the kitchen. Everyone but Mr. Wakefield, who continued to read his paper,

31

watched her closely as she walked over to the table and sat down in an empty chair. Lila's long hair, which was normally light brown and wavy, had plum-colored streaks in it and was straight as a board. Elizabeth glanced at her mother and her sister to see if they, too, had noticed that something awful had happened to Lila's hair. She could tell by their blank expressions that they had.

"That's all right," said Lila, helping herself to a piece of toast. "I'm in no hurry. I like to start slowly when I have a big day of shopping ahead of me."

Mrs. Wakefield cleared her throat. "Have you done something new to your hair, Lila?" she asked. "It looks . . . um . . . different."

Lila beamed. "Do you like it? I had it done yesterday afternoon. No one else has seen it yet."

"It's definitely very . . . striking," Elizabeth managed.

Alice Wakefield nodded. "It really brings out the color of your eyes, Lila."

Elizabeth noticed Jessica stuffing another spoonful of cereal into her mouth so that she didn't have to say anything.

Lila smiled smugly. "I wanted something really different," she told them. "Something that expresses the true me."

All of a sudden, Jessica got to her feet. "Let's go," she ordered, grabbing the bag that was hanging on the back of her chair. "Every minute spent here is a minute when we're not at the mall."

As soon as she heard Lila's lime-green Triumph start up, Elizabeth turned to her mother with a mischievous grin. "If that's the real Lila, she should have kept it a secret a little longer," she joked.

Mrs. Wakefield tried unsuccessfully to hide her own smile. "That hairdo makes Lila look like a Transylvanian," she admitted. "A very expensively dressed Transylvanian."

Elizabeth laughed. "She looks even weirder than a vampire, if you ask me. Vampires don't dye their hair funny colors." She shook her own golden hair. "I don't know why she didn't stick to her old style," she said. "Maybe she's coming down with this flu everybody's got and is delirious with fever."

"Yesterday in the bank I overheard someone talking about how many people are sick," Mrs. Wakefied said with a concerned expression. "Apparently nearly a quarter of your school has come down with it."

Elizabeth nodded. "Even Enid and Mr. Collins had to go home early yesterday afternoon," she explained. "It's bad enough not having my best friend around, but I don't know what I'm going to do if Mr. Collins is sick for long. I was really counting on his help with *The Oracle* while Penny's away."

Mrs. Wakefield sipped her coffee. "Let's just hope you and your sister don't get it," she said.

Elizabeth laughed. "You're just worried it'll make me do irrational things, like get my hair done so I look like a zombie."

All the way to the mall, Jessica tried to keep the conversation on any subject besides Lila's new hair-

33

style. Lila was too pretty ever to be unattractive, but Jessica had to admit that straight purple hair was really peculiar and unflattering.

So Jessica talked about the strange shade of green Bruce Patman had turned before he ran out of class the day before. She chatted about the great sale that was on at Lila's favorite shoe store in the Valley Mall. They even discussed their upcoming math test and whether or not it would be canceled if enough students were out with the flu.

Finally, however, Lila couldn't stand it anymore. "So tell me!" she demanded as they turned into the parking lot of the mall. "What do you *really* think?"

Jessica looked at her blankly. "About what?" she asked innocently.

Lila made a face. "About my hair, of course! I was really nervous about it at first, but Davina convinced me it was time to be bold and adventurous." She glanced at herself in the rearview mirror.

"Uh . . . yeah," Jessica said. "It really makes a statement." She sighed. "I wish I had the nerve to have something like that done to my hair. Something really *different*."

Lila pulled into a space near the main entrance. "Well, why don't you go see Davina?" she suggested. "I'm sure she could do wonders for you, too."

Jessica got out of the car. "I couldn't," she said with another wistful sigh. "My mother wouldn't let me spend the money. She still hasn't forgiven me for using the gas money for the Jeep on those velvet leggings two weeks ago. She thinks I'm extravagant."

Lila, climbed out of the Triumph. "Parents," she said with a shrug. "They just live on a different

34

planet, don't they?" She smiled **at Jessica** over the roof of the car.

Not only was Lila's hair **too straight**, Jessica decided, and a color that looked **much better** on fruit, but for some reason the style **made her** ears stick out. Jessica smiled back. *It's better than looking as though you come from another planet,* she thought.

"Did you see that?" Lila asked smugly. She tossed her hair over her shoulder. "Everybody's looking at me."

Jessica groaned inwardly. She had been trying very hard to forget about Lila's new hairstyle. Luckily, it was difficult to worry about how long it would take Lila's hair to get back to its natural color and texture when Jessica was busy trying to decide between the pink overalls and the patterned lilac leggings. Even so, she couldn't completely ignore the fact that other shoppers were nudging each other and glancing at Lila with amused expressions.

"It's lucky I'm used to being admired," Lila continued as Jessica paid for her purchase. "Or all this attention might go to my head."

Jessica grabbed her friend and gave her a shove toward the café. Somehow, she had to get her into a dark corner for a while. "Let's have lunch," she said urgently. "I'm really starved."

Lila stopped to glance at herself in a store window. "You know," she said thoughtfully, "I should have done this ages ago." She smiled at her reflection. "It makes me feel sorry for people who are ordinary."

"I think I'm going to have a cheeseburger," replied Jessica. "A cheeseburger and chili fries."

"It's too bad they don't serve caviar here," Lila commented as they entered the restaurant. "I'm in a caviar kind of mood."

Before Jessica could stop her, Lila made a beeline for a table in the center of the café. Several heads turned to watch her. Jessica was sure she could hear giggling and whispers.

Lila sat down and smiled. "I guess they've never seen anything like my hairstyle in Sweet Valley before."

"I'm sure they haven't," Jessica answered with complete honesty. She tried not to look around her. She was beginning to regret not going to the dirt bike race with Sam. Sitting in the middle of the restaurant like this made her nervous. Her only consolation was that every eye was on Lila and not on her.

"Did you see how the waitress was staring at my hair?" asked Lila after their orders had been taken. "She couldn't take her eyes off me."

Jessica hid her smile behind her water glass. "Um," she mumbled. "I noticed." Maybe they could go home right after lunch. There were still at least six of their favorite stores that they hadn't visited yet, but Jessica wasn't sure how much longer she could keep this up. If Lila didn't stop talking about her hair, Jessica might wind up telling her the truth.

As they were leaving the café a group of junior high school boys started laughing as they passed by.

"Where do you think that girl comes from?" one

of the boys asked in a voice loud enough to be heard at the other end of the mall. "Mars?"

A tiny frown appeared on Lila's perfect face. She turned to Jessica. "Who are they talking about?" she whispered.

But before Jessica could think of a reply, a small child standing in front of the card shop with his mother took one look at Lila and burst into tears.

Lila's eyes went from the crying child to the window behind him. In it she could see the grinning faces of several shoppers. She grabbed Jessica's arm. "Jessica," she hissed. "Those people behind us aren't laughing at *me*, are they?"

Jessica was caught off guard. "Well . . ." she said.

Lila's face froze as she began to realize the truth. "What do you mean, 'well'?"

A guilty look spread across Jessica's face. "I mean no," she corrected herself. "Of course they're not laughing at you."

But it was too late. Lila turned around suddenly to find one of the boys pointing at her. "They are!" she gasped. She turned on Jessica so quickly that Jessica dropped the bag containing her new lilac leggings. "Jessica Wakefield!" Lila's face was almost as purple as the streaks in her hair. "Jessica Wakefield, how could you. This is all your fault!"

"My fault?" squeaked Jessica. Leave it to Lila to blame her for this.

"And you call yourself my best friend!" Lila snapped. "Some best friend!"

Jessica tried to calm her down. "I don't know why you're getting so upset."

"You don't know why I'm getting so upset? Are you blind or something?"

"Lila, please," Jessica said in her most soothing voice. "You really are over—"

"My best friend!" Lila roared. "My best friend let me go out in public and make a complete fool of myself." She turned on her heel and rushed toward the car.

Jessica ran after her. "What did you want me to do?" she asked as she followed Lila across the parking lot. "Tell you that you look more like something from *Night of the Living Dead* than a Paris fashion show?"

Lila didn't answer.

"I didn't want to hurt your feelings," Jessica said, trying to catch her breath. "I was trying to be supportive."

Lila wrenched open the car door. "Thanks a bunch!" She threw herself into the driver's seat. "What good is a friend who doesn't tell you the truth?" she screamed. "If I wanted people to lie to me, I'd talk to my enemies!"

Jessica tried the door on her side, but it was locked. "Lila," she pleaded as the engine started. "Lila, let me in. We can discuss this calmly."

"You can *walk* back calmly," Lila snarled. "I don't give rides to Benedict Arnolds."

Great, thought Jessica as she watched the small green car drive away. *Here I am standing by myself on a Saturday afternoon as usual. Except there's no mud and no cute boy to drive me home.*

Elizabeth sat on the living room couch, her *Oracle* notebook open on the coffee table. She had been trying to work out her plan of action for the coming week, but she could already see the paper was going to be even more work than she had counted on, especially since Mr. Collins was sick with the flu. *Now, don't start getting discouraged*, she told herself sternly. *You can handle this and you know it*. She crossed her fingers. *As long as nothing goes wrong*.

At that moment her parents came home. Mr. Wakefield was whistling as he burst through the door.

Elizabeth looked up with a smile. "Well, you look happy," she said. "You must have gotten Grandma and Granddad a terrific gift!"

Mrs. Wakefield hung up her coat. "We got them a beautiful set of crystal glasses with a matching pitcher," she told Elizabeth. "I know it's just the kind of thing your grandmother loves."

Mr. Wakefield continued into the living room. "But that's not the best part," he announced with a grin. He put the packages he was carrying down on a chair. "Just wait till you see this, Elizabeth. It's going to knock your socks off."

Knock my socks off? That doesn't sound like Dad. Elizabeth looked at Mr. Wakefield in surprise. For a man who hated to shop, he seemed to have had an extremely good time.

She looked up at her mother, but for some reason Mrs. Wakefield wouldn't meet Elizabeth's eyes.

Elizabeth turned back to her father. She watched

with curiosity as he lifted a black box out of one of the shopping bags.

"Just wait till you see what I bought your mother!" he exclaimed. Mr. Wakefield slowly and carefully opened the box, as though he were unveiling a priceless work of art. He pulled back the tissue and lifted out a large glass sculpture of six thin, rodentlike creatures with enormous round eyes. They were standing on their hind legs and looking in different directions.

"Well?" Ned Wakefield said, beaming. "Don't just stand there—say something. Isn't it great?"

It was awful, even uglier than Lila's hair. Elizabeth looked to her mother for help, but her mother was staring at the sculpture with a fixed smile on her face.

"And I know just the place for it," Mr. Wakefield continued. He picked up the glass rodents and marched over to the mantel with them. "There!" he said. "That's perfect. That way no one who comes into the room can miss them."

"What are they?" Elizabeth asked, trying to sound interested.

Mr. Wakefield's smile grew even brighter. "Meerkats. Aren't they something?"

They were definitely something; Elizabeth just wasn't sure what.

"Meerkats live in the desert of southern Africa," explained Mrs. Wakefield, almost as though she had memorized this information. "They always band together and are among the most sociable animals in the world."

"Oh," said Elizabeth. "Isn't that fascinating?" She bent her head to conceal the smile tugging at her lips.

Mr. Wakefield stepped back. "They really add something to the room," he decided. "Walk a few feet away, Elizabeth. It's almost as though their eyes are following you."

Elizabeth did as she was told. "Gee, they really do, don't they?" Elizabeth glanced at her mother. She could tell from the expression on her face that she shared Elizabeth's opinion that although meerkats were probably very nice in the Kalahari Desert, they weren't so appealing in a California living room.

"I'm just going to go get a cloth and give these little guys a polish," Mr. Wakefield said. "Don't move! I'll be right back."

Elizabeth exploded into a muffled giggle as soon as her father left the room.

"I couldn't stop him," her mother quickly whispered, rolling her eyes. "He fell in love with them."

"But why can't he keep them in his study?" Elizabeth whispered back. "You know, where no one else would have to look at them?"

Her mother shook her head. "He wants the world to see them," she said. "And besides, he bought them as a gift for me."

Elizabeth and her mother gazed at the meerkats in silence for a few seconds, then burst out laughing.

"So where are we meeting Lila and her date?" Sam asked as Jessica got into his car.

"We're not." She leaned over and gave him a kiss. "Lila's not coming with us tonight."

Sam raised one eyebrow. "Don't tell me you two had another fight," he kidded. "What was it about this time? Which one of you has the best taste in socks?"

Jessica gave him a look. Sam was completely wonderful in almost every way, except that he had an excellent memory for some of the lower moments in her and Lila's friendship.

"I wish," she said flatly. "This time she's really mad at me." Carefully avoiding any mention of shopping or the mall, Jessica proceeded to tell Sam about Lila's new hairstyle. "What do you think?" she asked when she was finished. "Do you think I should have told her the truth?"

Sam's warm laugh filled the car. "I can see your point," he admitted. "Lila isn't the kind of person who appreciates total honesty."

Jessica clapped her hands in triumph. "You see? That's exactly what I thought."

"On the other hand, if you thought people might make fun of her, maybe it would've been better to say something."

"Are you kidding?" Jessica's voice was shrill with disbelief. "Lila would have killed me."

Sam shook his head. "I guess what you have to ask yourself is whether you would have wanted Lila to tell you the truth in the same situation."

Jessica frowned in thought. Would she have wanted Lila to tell her the truth? She could picture the sugary smile on Lila's face and hear the patronizing tone in her voice. *Well, I guess it's not that bad,*

Lila would say. *If you don't mind looking like someone who couldn't get a date on an army base in the Antarctic, that is.*

"No," Jessica decided, "I'd definitely want Lila to lie."

Four

"Come on," Todd coaxed. "Just come to the cafeteria for fifteen minutes."

"How many times do I have to tell you?" Elizabeth snapped, her usual air of calm and control completely gone. "I don't have time."

"Hey," he said, "Don't get mad at me. *I'm* not making everyone sick."

Elizabeth smiled and leaned her head against his shoulder. "I'm sorry I'm in such a bad mood. I just don't know how much more I can handle." It was already Tuesday, and now over a third of the school was out with the flu. The paper was short-handed, and everyone was working extra hard to get that week's issue ready by Wednesday afternoon. But no one was working harder than Elizabeth. Only the fear that *The Oracle* wouldn't come out at all kept her from collapsing from exhaustion—or just giving up altogether.

"You have to eat something," Todd said. "You can't work like this on an empty stomach."

Elizabeth smiled. "You sound like my mother," she joked. But then her voice became serious again. "The truth is, though, that I just don't have time. On top of everything else, I have to finish the events column. I convinced Robin Wilson to do it because she used to write for *The Oracle*, but she only got as far as next Monday and then she came down with the dreaded illness."

"Look at the bright side," Todd said with a smile. "The way things are going, by next Tuesday there isn't going to be anyone left at school to go anywhere. You might as well relax."

"I wish I could." She shook her head. "I just don't know what I'll do if anybody else gets sick. I'm already struggling to fill all the space."

"I'd help you myself," Todd offered, "but I think you may be better off without me. Even my mother has noticed my lack of writing ability, and she thinks I'm perfect."

Elizabeth gave Todd a hug. "I'll let you know if I get really desperate."

Todd laughed. "If you get *really* desperate, you could always run a contest to name this flu."

Rod Sullivan leaned across the lunch table and waved his hand in front of Olivia's eyes. "Hello in there. Anybody home?" he said.

Olivia, who had been staring across the cafeteria to where Todd Wilkins, Scott Trost, and Winston

Egbert were all having lunch together, smiled at him. "I was noticing that Elizabeth isn't at lunch again today," she said with a sigh. "It's a shame that *The Oracle*'s best writers are all home sick. I'm sure that's why she's working so hard."

"You think she needs some help?"

Olivia nodded. "I know she does, but I'm already doing an extra piece, plus I've got so much to do for *Visions*. . . ." Her voice trailed off. There was one other reason she wasn't doing more for the paper: Elizabeth hadn't asked for her help. But she wasn't going to mention that to Rod.

Rod touched her hand. "Give yourself a break," he advised. "You know you're doing more than your share." He looked thoughtful for a second. "Maybe there's something I can do, though."

Olivia laughed. "Rod," she said gently, "I know you mean well, but Elizabeth has really high standards. Let's face it, your writing isn't going to impress her." Secretly she was glad about that—knowing how much Rod admired Elizabeth, Olivia wouldn't have been very comfortable if Rod spent a lot of time alone with her.

Rod leaned back in his chair. "Well, thanks for the vote of confidence," he said, sulking.

Olivia punched him playfully. "Oh, don't be like that. You're a brilliant artist, Rod. But you trying to help Elizabeth with writing and editing *The Oracle* would be like a cat trying to help a fish swim."

"Oh yeah?" asked Rod.

Olivia threw her napkin at him. "Yeah."

* * *

Amy Sutton took a sip of her apple juice and wrinkled her nose. "I hope I'm not getting sick," she said. "This juice tastes really funny." She held the container out to Jessica, who was sitting beside her in the cafeteria. "Take a taste, will you, Jess? See if it's me or it."

Lila looked up, smiling one of her nastiest smiles. "I wouldn't ask Jessica if I were you," she said sweetly. "Even if it was curdling, she'd tell you it was fine."

Jessica sighed. Lila had gone back to Davina on Saturday afternoon and had her hair dyed back to its natural color. Since then, she had more or less started speaking to Jessica again, but things between them were worse than when she hadn't been speaking to her at all. Lila managed to get a dig in at Jessica and her lack of honesty at every opportunity, and when there wasn't any opportunity she made one.

Jessica turned her blue-green eyes on her best friend. "Why don't you get off my case?" she asked, equally sweetly. "I said I was sorry. What more can I do?"

Lila stared back at her in mock surprise. "I don't know what you're talking about," she said. "I'm not on your case. I was only trying to point out to Amy that you can trust a thief, but you can't trust a liar."

Jessica banged her fork on the table. "What are you talking about, Lila? I am not a thief or a liar," she said indignantly. "Anyway, there's a big difference between lying and trying to spare someone's feelings."

Lila turned to Caroline Pearce. "Who can you

trust if you can't trust your best friend?" she asked. "That's what I'd like to know."

Caroline, a major gossip, who didn't have that close a relationship with the truth herself, shook her head in total bewilderment. "I don't know. Do you know, Amy?"

Amy shrugged.

"Oh, come on, you guys," snapped Jessica. "Are you trying to tell me that none of you has ever fibbed a little for a good cause?"

Lila tossed her head in her usual haughty way, and her hair swung stiffly. "I haven't," she said archly. "Not when it was a matter of life or death. I happen to pride myself on my incredible honesty, as a matter of fact."

Jessica bit her lip to stop herself from getting into even more trouble. *If Lila is incredibly honest*, she said silently to herself, *then the moon is made of green cheese.*

Amy nodded. "Me, too," she said. "I might stretch the truth a little over something teensy. But when it comes to things that really affect a person's life, I agree that honesty is the best policy." She smiled sympathetically at Lila, who had told her and anyone else who would listen the whole story of Saturday in elaborate detail. "No matter how much the truth hurts, it never hurts as much as being deceived."

Jessica groaned. "You sound like a fortune cookie."

"I'm with Amy," Caroline said. "I might fib a little over something that didn't matter, but not over something *really* important, like hair."

49

Jessica looked from one girl to the next. She picked up her fork again and speared a piece of potato. *Maybe they're right*, she thought. *Maybe always trying to spare people's feelings isn't really what they want.*

As soon as school was over, Elizabeth raced to the *Oracle* office to finish the events column and start editing the few articles that had been handed in. She was hunched over her typewriter when she heard a knock on the door.

"Elizabeth?" Jennifer Mitchell poked her head through the door. "Can I talk to you for a minute?"

Now what? Elizabeth wondered with a sigh. "Don't tell me," she said, managing a small laugh. "Your article's going to be late."

Jennifer came into the room, shutting the door behind her. "It's not going to be late," she said with a shake of her head. Her voice was hoarse and strained. "It's not going to happen at all."

Elizabeth looked at Jennifer more closely. Her eyes were glassy and her cheeks were so red they might be on fire. "Oh no!" she cried. "Don't tell me you're sick, too!" She wanted to sympathize with Jennifer, but she couldn't quite keep the despair out of her own voice. Jennifer was supposed to write the lead feature for page one.

"I'm afraid so," Jennifer whispered. "I can hardly stand up, Liz. I have to go home and go to bed."

Elizabeth ran a hand through her hair. *Get a grip on yourself*, she ordered. *Jennifer's about to fall over.* "You're absolutely right," she said with genuine concern. "You look awful."

50

"I'm really sorry, but there's just no way I can finish my piece now. Maybe if I'm feeling better in the morning . . ."

"Don't be ridiculous." Elizabeth got to her feet and went over to put her hand on Jennifer's forehead. She was burning hot. "No article is as important as your health. Forget about the paper and go home and take care of yourself."

Jennifer was obviously relieved. "Are you sure? I hate to let you down like this."

Gently but firmly, Elizabeth turned Jennifer around. "You're not letting anybody down," she assured her. "It's not a problem. Really. I have a couple of half-finished pieces of my own in a drawer somewhere. I'll just use one of them."

Once Jennifer was gone, Elizabeth slumped back in her chair with a groan. There were no half-finished pieces of her own anywhere. In fact, she was three articles short for that week's issue. "What am I going to do?" she moaned out loud. There was simply no way she could put the paper together *and* write three extra pieces at the same time. Not by the next afternoon. She smiled sourly. *Never mind being the first editor-in-chief of a high school newspaper ever to receive the Pulitzer Prize*, she told herself. *You'll be lucky if you're not the first editor-in-chief in the history of Sweet Valley High not to publish a paper at all.*

Elizabeth stared at the page in her typewriter, trying to think. There was a chance that she could get Jessica to write something. She had once done a very funny piece on the worst dates she had ever been on. If Jessica could be persuaded to help out, that would leave Elizabeth with only two blanks to fill. She bit her lip. Maybe Todd's idea of running a contest to name the flu wasn't as silly as it had sounded. At least it would take up space. And if she could get him to put it together himself, that would free her to do other things.

"Oh, sure," she muttered out loud. "That'll give you plenty of time to do the editing, lay out the paper, *and* write a feature story for the first page."

"Talking to yourself now?" asked a voice behind her. "That's a real bad sign."

Elizabeth jumped. She had been so preoccupied with her problems that she hadn't heard Rod Sullivan come into the office. As soon as she turned around his sunny smile vanished.

"Hey, what's wrong?" he asked immediately. "You look like you've lost your best friend."

"Not permanently," said Elizabeth. She made a face. "She just has the flu. She and everybody else in this school."

Rod pulled a chair over and sat down beside her. "What happened? Another intrepid reporter go down with the Sweet Valley plague?"

She nodded. "Jennifer Mitchell, my feature writer. I just don't know what I'm going to do," she confided. "If only Mr. Collins weren't sick, I could ask him to do some of the editing while I wrote Jennifer's piece . . ."

Rod grinned good-naturedly. "You could hope that the printer catches this bug by tomorrow. Then there wouldn't be any problem."

Elizabeth had to smile. "Stop trying to cheer me up," she said. "With my luck, the printer's the one person in Sweet Valley who's immune to this flu."

Rod put a hand on her shoulder. "I'll do better than cheer you up," he answered. "I'll write that feature article myself."

She couldn't hide her surprise. "*You?*" Elizabeth stared at him. "But you're not a writer, Rod. You're an artist."

"Hey, don't knock it. I'm not saying I'm Ernest Hemingway, but I can form simple sentences and get my point across."

Rod was going to save her! It almost didn't matter how well he wrote as long as he wrote in English. If he handed in something that was reasonable, she could make it work. Elizabeth had always liked Rod, but never so much as she did right then. Overwhelmed with relief, she threw her arms around him. "Thank you!" For the first time all day she felt as though she really could cope after all. She smiled at Rod. "What else can I say but thank you?"

His eyes met hers. "Thank you will do just fine for now," he said softly. "Especially if I get another hug when I turn in my piece."

Rod was looking at her so seriously that for an instant a slight feeling of discomfort ran through Elizabeth. But then he laughed, and she realized he had only been kidding around.

"You can have two hugs," she said, laughing herself. "And if it's really good, you can have three!"

Elizabeth knew that the best way to get her sister to do something usually involved blackmail—blackmail or bribery. Unfortunately, at the moment she didn't have anything with which to blackmail or bribe Jessica, so she decided to throw herself on her sister's mercy instead.

Jessica sat in the *Oracle* office listening to Elizabeth's tragic story, a faraway look in her eyes. Elizabeth couldn't decide whether the vague expression on her twin's face meant that she was actually thinking about writing something for *The Oracle*, or that she was mulling over what to wear to school the next day.

"Well?" Elizabeth asked anxiously when she had finished her pitch. "What do you think?"

Jessica nodded. "Sure," she said. "I'll do it right after dinner."

Elizabeth couldn't believe her ears. "You will? You'll write a piece by tomorrow?"

Jessica nodded again. "Yeah. I don't have any homework because half my teachers are out, and Sam's got a date with his spark plugs tonight, so I have nothing else to do."

"But you realize that I have to have it by tomorrow morning, right? You're really going to have to think of something fast."

Jessica waved away her concern. "Think of something? Are you kidding? I'm absolutely inspired."

"You are?" Usually the only thing that inspired Jessica was a sale or a very cute boy.

"Uh-huh." Jessica gave her sister a satisfied smile. "I'm going to write an anonymous piece entitled 'To Tell the Truth,' about whether or not honesty really is the best policy. What do you think?"

Elizabeth threw her arms around her twin. "I think you're a genius."

* * *

Olivia sat back, studying the poster she had made asking for contributions to the new issue of *Visions*. It looked totally professional, if she said so herself. She tilted her head first to one side and then to the other. Maybe she should make the heading stand out more. She frowned. She wasn't sure how she could do that now without having to redo the entire thing.

Olivia snapped her fingers. Rod was the graphics expert. He would know. She smiled at herself in the mirror as she went to the phone. Not only would Rod know what to do, but it gave her an excuse to talk to him. They had both been so busy lately that even though he still drove her to school every morning and ate lunch with her almost every afternoon, she felt as though she hardly saw him.

"I can't talk right now," Rod said when she explained her problem. "I have to finish my article for *The Oracle.*"

"What?" Olivia asked, dumbfounded. Rod's least favorite subject was English, and the only books he had ever read that weren't for school were books on art and design. The most she had ever seen him write was a note to his mother telling her he was going to be late getting back from school, and that usually contained mistakes. "You're writing an article for *The Oracle?*"

"Yeah. Your lack of faith in me at lunch today made me want to prove something," he said. "And when I saw Elizabeth in the office she looked so downtrodden that I had to offer." A note of pride crept into his voice. "Elizabeth jumped at the idea, believe it or not. She didn't think it was ridiculous at all."

"I think it's nice of you to give her a hand and everything," Olivia said. "I'm just a little surprised. I mean, you've never shown the tiniest bit of interest in writing before."

Rod laughed. "Oh, come on, Olivia. You know how interested I am in journalism. It's poetry and stuff like that that I'm not really into."

Olivia made a face. "Well, I certainly don't want to take up any more of your precious time," she said, sounding a little cooler than she had intended. She couldn't shake the feeling that Rod wouldn't have been half so helpful if it had been Penny Ayala who was having a hard time. Or herself, for that matter.

"Look, Olivia," Rod said quickly, "as soon as I finish this, we'll work out what to do about your poster, OK?"

"Sure," Olivia said, wishing she didn't feel so petty toward Elizabeth. "Call me back when you've finished your masterpiece."

Elizabeth crossed her fingers as she walked to the *Oracle* office on Wednesday morning. In her book bag she had Jessica's hilarious piece on honesty and the name-the-flu contest that Todd had put together. If Rod had anything to give her—anything at all—she should be able to make the printer's deadline. *Don't get your hopes up too much,* she advised herself. *Rod meant well, but he might not have realized how much work there is in writing a feature.*

Elizabeth turned down the corridor and came to a stop. There, leaning against the door to the office, was Rod Sullivan. He had an enormous smile on his face and several sheets of typing paper in his hand. He waved them in greeting.

"Don't tell me you finished it!" she cried, hurrying toward him.

He handed it to her with a flourish. "It's all yours," he said, obviously pleased with himself. "I didn't have any trouble that staying up till two in the morning couldn't solve."

Elizabeth grabbed the article and stood there reading it quickly. It was good! In fact, it was better than good. It was very good. She had been afraid she might have to rewrite the entire thing, but she couldn't find even a spelling mistake. It reminded her vaguely of something she had read before, but she didn't have the time to think of what that was. In any case, what did it matter? All beginning writers imitated the styles of writers they admired. That was often how people learned to write in the first place.

"Well?" asked Rod anxiously. "What do you think?"

Elizabeth shook her head, still reading. "I can't believe this," she replied. "I had no idea you were such a good writer." She looked at him with a smile. "This is great."

Rod came closer, looking over her shoulder. "I think reading your features and seeing how hard you work has inspired me," he said.

Realizing he was completely serious, Elizabeth flushed. She turned to face him. "I don't know about that," she said, "but I do know that the first article I wrote wasn't this good."

"I bet you say that to all the guys," he said with a laugh.

Almost dizzy with relief, Elizabeth laughed, too. "Only the ones named Ernest Hemingway."

Elizabeth hummed to herself as she put the finishing touches on *The Oracle* that afternoon. She couldn't believe how much fun she was having, or how relaxed she felt. She looked over at Rod, who was pasting the last piece of copy into place. She couldn't have done it without him. Not only had his expert advice on layout and design saved her hours, but his good humor had turned a difficult job into an enjoyable one. She hadn't felt this happy since she'd watched Penny Ayala leave for the airport on Friday morning.

"That's it!" Rod did a little dance step. "We're ready to roll!"

Elizabeth smiled. "I really don't know how to thank you. This is service above and beyond the call of duty. If it weren't for you—"

He held up one hand. "Please, I'm a modest man." His smile became serious. "And anyway, Elizabeth, I was glad to do it."

Impulsively, Elizabeth leaned over and kissed him on the cheek. "You're too much," she said.

"You're too much, too," he said in a low voice.

He was looking into her eyes so intently that for a second she thought he was going to kiss her back. Instinctively, she stepped aside.

Rod immediately made a silly face and moved in

the opposite direction. "We can't keep meeting like this," he joked, waggling his eyebrows. "Hey, I have an idea. Why don't you and Todd and Olivia and I all go out together Saturday night? Then we can really celebrate."

Elizabeth laughed, feeling relieved. Of course Rod hadn't been thinking of kissing her. He was Olivia's boyfriend. "I can't think of anything I'd rather do more," she said.

Five

Jessica was looking even prettier than usual as she
made her way to the cafeteria on Friday afternoon.
*There's nothing like being praised and admired to make a
girl look her best*, she thought as she strode along.
That week's issue of *The Oracle* had been out for
only a few hours, but already everyone was talking
about the article she had anonymously written, "To
Tell the Truth." She had heard students discussing
it between classes. She had heard girls arguing
about it in the bathroom. Even her English teacher,
whose only interest in her writing seemed to be
scrawling comments in red pencil all over it, had
read the *Oracle* piece aloud to the class, and then
spent the whole period discussing it. "Funny and
thought-provoking," he had called it.

Jessica sailed over to the lunch line, bought some

lasagna, and went over to the table where Amy, Jean West, and Caroline were sitting.

"Have you seen this?" Amy asked as Jessica slid into the chair beside her. She held up a copy of *The Oracle*.

Jessica nodded. "Who hasn't?" She smiled. "It's all anybody seems to be talking about."

"It's true," Jean said. "It really makes you think, doesn't it?" She shook her head. "I wish the author would just come out and tell us which is right and which is wrong, though. I have to admit, I have a really hard time telling people the truth when I know it's something they don't want to hear."

Caroline shrugged. "Who cares whether they want to hear it?" she said. "You know, people are always getting on my case for being a gossip, but since I've been thinking about this honesty thing I've realized that I'm not a gossip, I'm a spreader of truth."

A smile flickered across the faces of the other girls. "Not always," Amy said, with a look at Jessica and Jean. "Sometimes you're just a spreader of gossip."

"Excuse *me*," said Caroline frostily.

They all looked up when they heard the loud, sure voice of Lila Fowler over the din of the cafeteria. She plunked herself into the seat across from Jessica and tossed a copy of *The Oracle* onto the table. "Admit it!" she ordered, leaning forward and pointing to the headline "To Tell the Truth: Is Honesty Really the Best Policy?" "You wrote that, didn't you, Jessica?"

The other girls turned to Jessica in surprise.

"I cannot tell a lie," Jessica said with a laugh. "I did!"

Lila smiled triumphantly. "I knew it!"

"So you liked my piece?" Jessica prodded.

"As far as it went, yes," Lila said. She reached into her shoulder bag and pulled out a glossy women's magazine. "But I think you're still a little confused." She handed the magazine to Jessica. "Here, read this. It should convince you once and for all that I'm right."

Jessica stared down at the cover. In large red letters it said: "Learn How to Unlock the Totally Honest You!"

"Well, what do you think?" Elizabeth stood behind her parents while they looked through the copies of *The Oracle* she had brought home for them the day before.

"It looks terrific," Mr. Wakefield said. "Very professional."

Mrs. Wakefield smiled at her. "No one would ever know that you produced it with a fraction of the usual staff and no adviser at all," she added.

A warm feeling of well-being went through Elizabeth. She felt proud of herself and thankful to Rod, Jessica, and Todd for the fact that *The Oracle* had come out not only on time but with all its pages filled.

"I hope you're not going to spend the whole weekend working on next week's issue," Mrs. Wakefield said. "You deserve a break."

"And I'm taking one," Elizabeth assured her. "I'm not going to think of the paper even once today. I'm going to work on some poems."

Mrs. Wakefield smiled. "What a lovely idea."

"That's nice, honey," said Mr. Wakefield, returning his attention to his pancakes.

Elizabeth sat down beside Jessica, who hadn't said one word since coming down to breakfast. She was poring over an article in a woman's magazine with obvious fascination.

"Olivia Davidson came up with a brilliant idea for *Visions*," Elizabeth explained to her mother. "She's doing an issue completely devoted to the environment. You know, endangered species, the rain forests, and how beautiful the earth could be. That kind of thing." She poured herself some juice. "I'd really like to write something special for it. Something no one else has thought of."

Mr. Wakefield froze in the act of pouring more syrup on his pancakes. A joyous smile lit up his face. "I know just the thing!" he exclaimed, putting the syrup down. "Why don't you write about meerkats?"

Elizabeth stared at her father in silence. He was as excited as a man who had just discovered a diamond in the sugar bowl, as excited as a man who polished his meerkat statue at least once a day.

"They're wonderful creatures, environmentally speaking," Mr. Wakefield went on. "You couldn't do better than meerkats." He shook his head. "*And* they're a very neglected species."

Not daring to catch her mother's eye, Elizabeth smiled back at her father. "What a good idea," she said. "I'll certainly think about it, Dad." *But not for long*, she added to herself.

*   *   *

Olivia was in a good mood on Saturday afternoon. Because so many people were out of school, she had had less homework to deal with that week, which meant that she'd had more time to devote to her own poetry, as well as to her plans for the next issue of *Visions*.

She was in such a good mood, in fact, that she was really looking forward to the double date she and Rod were going on with Elizabeth and Todd that night. A few days earlier, the thought of spending an evening with Elizabeth would have made her anxious. She would have been worried that Rod would be comparing her to Elizabeth and finding her lacking. But not anymore. She sang to herself as she chose the dress she would wear. She laughed as she whipped up an oatmeal face mask. She danced through the bathroom with her favorite pink towel in one hand and her special bath oil in the other. *Just because Elizabeth's terrific doesn't mean I'm not terrific, too*, she told herself. She got out her manicure set, her tweezers, and her eyelash curler. *And just because you're terrific now doesn't mean you're not going to look more terrific later*, she told her reflection.

Hours later, Olivia was still in the bathroom when she heard her mother calling up the stairs. "Olivia! Olivia! Rod's here!"

Olivia studied herself in the full-length mirror. She didn't just look good, she looked great. Her curly brown hair was perfect, framing her pretty face like a cloud. Her dress was a traffic-stopper. Her wildly patterned tights were eye-catching and sophisticated. She dared Rod to look at her and even remember Elizabeth Wakefield's name.

"Mirror, mirror on the wall," Olivia said, grinning at herself with delight. "Who is the fairest, most original dresser, and generally most wonderful of them all?"

"Olivia!" her mother yelled. "Olivia! Did you hear me? Rod's here!"

"I'm coming!" Olivia shouted back. She gave herself one last glance. "You look like a million dollars," she told herself with a laugh. "Two million," she corrected. "Two million dollars and a Caribbean cruise."

Olivia was thrilled when she saw the look on Rod's face. "Wow!" He gave a low whistle. "You look fantastic, Liv."

"Do you really think so?" she asked, trying not to sound too pleased with herself.

"Yeah." He tilted his head to one side. "Doesn't Elizabeth have a dress like that?"

Olivia froze. "Elizabeth?" All of a sudden she felt some of her self-confidence evaporating.

Rod was nodding. "Yeah," he said. "Only hers is blue."

Olivia was still feeling pretty good about herself as they drove to the movie. Rod chatted excitedly the entire way about how well that week's issue of *The Oracle* had turned out and about his page-one byline.

"You didn't think I could do it, did you?" he asked as they pulled into a parking space.

Olivia leaned over and gave him a kiss. "No," she said. "But I was wrong." Though she had only had a chance to read through Rod's piece very quickly, it really was good.

"At least Elizabeth had more faith in me than you did," Rod said.

More of Olivia's self-confidence seemed to vanish into the air.

When Olivia saw Elizabeth and Todd, her confidence level slipped again. Elizabeth looked stunning. People were turning their heads to catch another glimpse of her as they entered the theater. Elizabeth and Todd had obviously spent the afternoon at the beach, and had come out without going home first to change. Elizabeth was wearing shorts and a sweatshirt, and her damp hair was pulled into a loose ponytail. Olivia touched her own hair. She'd had to torture it for hours to make it behave, and all Elizabeth had had to do was dunk hers in salt water and tie it back with a piece of pink terry cloth. She wasn't even wearing any makeup. No makeup, old clothes, and wet hair. Olivia felt as though she had turned up for tennis in an evening gown.

"You look gorgeous!" Elizabeth said to her. She laughed. "Now I wish I'd gone home and put on something nice. Look at me! I feel like a real slob."

"You don't look like a slob," Rod said quickly. "You look like Aphrodite just risen from the sea."

Aphrodite? Olivia looked over at him. It would never have occurred to her that Rod even knew who Aphrodite was.

Elizabeth rolled her eyes. "I don't think Aphrodite wore a sweatshirt and sneakers," she said with a grin.

"She would have if she'd seen you," said Rod.

Olivia had to stop herself from kicking him.

By the time the movie was over and they were all sitting in a corner booth at the Dairi Burger, Olivia no longer wanted to kick Rod. She wanted to murder him.

Olivia felt invisible. Since they arrived at the Dairi Burger no one had said more than a few words to her. Instead, Rod and Todd were listening to Elizabeth's stories of her disastrous first week as editor-in-chief. As awful as she made it sound, Elizabeth also made it sound incredibly funny. Neither of the boys could stop laughing.

"You should have seen her after Jennifer went home with the flu," Rod said when he caught his breath. He imitated Elizabeth sitting at her desk, talking to herself.

Todd almost choked on his soda. "I knew it had to be bad if she asked *me* to help her out," he said. "My writing skills are just a little better than my stone-cutting skills."

Olivia forced herself to smile. It wasn't the world's most sincere smile, but at least the corners of her mouth were turned up. "It sounds absolutely horrible," she commented.

No one heard her.

"I don't know what I would have done without Rod," Elizabeth said. She gave him a warm and happy smile that made her look even prettier. "You really saved my life."

"Don't even mention it," he said. "You're an editor who commands loyalty."

Olivia felt like throwing up. *Oh, give me a break,* she thought, spearing a french fry with her fork. How could Rod, *her* Rod, a boy she liked and admired so much, behave like such a complete clown? He had never been like this before. She looked over at Rod, who was gazing at Elizabeth with a stupid grin. *It's her fault*, said a jealous little voice inside her head. *He was never like this before.* Olivia pushed her plate away, looking from Elizabeth to Rod.

"I don't understand what you're so mad about," Rod said as Olivia slammed the car door shut.

She marched up the path to her house, Rod hurrying to catch up. "No, you wouldn't," she snapped. "You paid no attention to me all night, why should you know?"

His hand caught her elbow and pulled her to a stop. "Olivia, please. You were so quiet and sulky that it was hard to talk to you. If you'd just tell me what's wrong—"

Olivia turned to face him. Somehow, standing in front of her own house, alone with Rod, it was hard to say why she was so angry. Because Elizabeth had looked so pretty? Because she was funny and interesting? Because Rod liked her? It wasn't as if he had gone out with Elizabeth on his own, was it? The four of them had been together all night. Maybe Rod was right. Maybe if Olivia had been a little more talkative herself . . .

He put his arms around her. "What is it, Olivia? If you don't tell me, how am I going to know?"

She leaned against his shoulder. It was no use; the truth—that she was jealous of the attention he had given Elizabeth—sounded stupid. Todd had spent quite a lot of time talking to her about the rain forests, and neither Rod nor Elizabeth had been upset by that. "It's nothing," she said at last. "I guess I'm just feeling a little tired, that's all. It's been a busy week."

Jessica was in a thoughtful mood as she got ready for bed that night. Every word of the article Lila had given her had stayed in Jessica's mind all day. She had thought about the article while she was at the race with Sam. She had thought about it while she was dancing with him at the party they'd gone to that evening. She had even thought about it while Sam was kissing her good night—and she usually didn't think of anything when Sam was kissing her but the kiss itself.

Jessica stared into the bathroom mirror, pointing her toothbrush at her image. " 'A more honest you,' " she said, quoting from the article, " 'a you who is loved not just because you're beautiful but because you are a person of exceptional character and integrity, too.' "

Jessica found the idea appealing. After all, everybody was always teasing her about being flighty and frivolous—even Lila and Amy, who were certainly more flighty and frivolous than she was. And her parents were always encouraging Jessica to be more responsible. "You won't be sixteen forever, you know," her mother was always telling her. "You're going to have to grow up sometime." Even Elizabeth nagged her about taking things more seriously. If she became totally honest, they would have to leave her alone.

Jessica finished brushing her teeth and went back to her room. There were other advantages to telling the truth, she decided. For one thing, it would save her hours of making up excuses. For another thing, if she always told people the truth, there wouldn't be any more of those awful moments when she found herself caught in a white lie.

She climbed into bed. It was obvious from the response to her own piece that almost everyone agreed that one hundred percent honesty was the best policy. Everyone at the party had thought so, too. Only Sam seemed to think it was all right to bend the truth now and then.

"Let's face it," he had said while they were discussing the issue with some of their friends. "If I ask Jess whether or not she thinks I'm a better rider than some other guy on the track, I don't want her to tell me no. I want her to lie." Everybody had laughed about what a big ego he had.

Jessica turned off the bedside lamp. As she closed her eyes she remembered something Elizabeth had said: *Oh, what a tangled web we weave, when first we practice to deceive . . .*

She fell asleep vowing never to weave herself a tangled web again.

Six

By Monday morning Jessica was feeling happy and determined. She had made her decision. She was going to become honest. She would put George Washington to shame. She, Jessica Wakefield, was going to become the most truthful person the world had ever seen. From that morning on, when people asked her for her opinion they were going to get it. No more trying to be nice. No more trying to spare the feelings of others. From that morning on, she would say exactly what she thought.

If she didn't want to go to a race with Sam, she wouldn't make up some lame excuse. She would tell him the truth. "Sam, I don't want to go," she'd say. "I'd rather watch a tank of goldfish for the whole afternoon." If she didn't like the dress Lila was wearing, she wouldn't say something wishy-washy about the fabric or the color. No, she would look Lila right in the eye and say, "Lila, that dress looks like something my father would pick out."

Jessica jumped out of bed. Life was going to be a lot less complicated. There would be no more excuses to keep track of, no more lies to keep straight. As Jessica stood at the window, looking out at the sunshine, she felt free. There had been times in the past when she had told so many different people so many different versions of the truth that she couldn't remember which was which. There had been times when she had talked herself into such a corner that she'd had to rely on Elizabeth to get her back out. But never again. Jessica smiled at the blue sky over the rooftops of Sweet Valley, feeling like a new person.

Elizabeth was already at breakfast by the time the new, honest Jessica Wakefield came down. "Good morning, everyone," Jessica said to her mother and her sister. "How are you on this beautiful day?"

Mrs. Wakefield gazed at her over her coffee cup. She had a "now what?" expression on her face.

"You're just in time," Elizabeth said. "I was about to read Mom the poem I wrote for *Visions*." She looked at Mrs. Wakefield. "Todd helped me with it. It's called 'The Last Days of the Amazon.' "

Jessica groaned out loud. Elizabeth really was too much. Only her sister would think of writing a poem called "The Last Days of the Amazon." Why didn't she write a poem about something people were really interested in? "An Afternoon at the Mall," for instance.

Elizabeth's voice lost a little of its enthusiasm. "Do you have some problem with the title?" she asked, glaring at her twin over the page in her hand.

Jessica reached for the cereal. This was wonderful. She didn't have to pretend for even one second that she was interested in Elizabeth's boring poem about a bunch of trees and a river. "It sounds like the title of a documentary," she said.

Her mother gave her a warning look.

"Well, you don't have to listen, then," Elizabeth snapped. "Mom's interested, even if you aren't." She cleared her throat. " 'The Last Days of the Amazon,' " she repeated. She glanced at her mother, and then she began to read.

Jessica tried not to listen, but it was difficult since she was sitting just a few feet away from the poet herself. Even though Jessica tried to concentrate on thinking about herself and how much more popular she was going to be now that she had so much character and integrity, parts of her sister's poem interrupted her thoughts—lines about insects and ozone.

"Why, that's beautiful," Mrs. Wakefield said when Elizabeth was done. "That really is beautiful. I'm sure Olivia will want to publish it."

Elizabeth was pleased. "Do you really think so? You're sure it's not too long?"

Jessica watched her mother's face. She could tell from the way Mrs. Wakefield was smiling that she did think the poem was too long, though probably not as long as Jessica thought it was. Jessica, in fact, would have been happy to see the whole thing thrown in the garbage.

"I think it's perfect," Mrs. Wakefield said. "I wouldn't change a word."

I'd change about a hundred and fifty words, Jessica thought.

"I'm really glad you think so," said Elizabeth. "I've worked really hard on it. I think it's almost there."

The old Jessica would have put another spoonful of cereal into her mouth and not said anything. The new Jessica raised her eyes and said, "Where, exactly, is 'there' supposed to be? It sounded like a nursery rhyme to me. A nursery rhyme about bugs."

Elizabeth turned to her slowly. "For your information, it does not sound like a nursery rhyme. If you knew anything about poetry, you'd know that."

Jessica made a face. "Pardon me for breathing, but I don't have to be an English professor to know when I don't like something." She picked up her glass. "I was only giving you my honest opinion, you know. I thought writers wanted constructive criticism."

Elizabeth stuck the poem in her folder. "Well, who asked you for your honest opinion?" she snapped. "There is a difference between constructive criticism and having no idea what you're talking about."

Jessica watched her sister stomp out of the room.

"I think you could have been a little kinder," Mrs. Wakefield said when Elizabeth was gone.

"The truth isn't always kind," Jessica said wisely.

Suddenly she heard the engine of the Jeep start up. "I don't believe this!" she wailed, throwing her napkin down. "She's leaving without me!"

"I guess sisters aren't always kind, either," Mrs. Wakefield said as Jessica raced for the door.

There was good news and bad news waiting for Elizabeth when she reached school that Monday morning. The good news was that both Enid and Mr. Collins were feeling better and were back at school. Elizabeth had really missed having Enid to talk to the week before, when everything had been so hectic; and she had certainly missed having Mr. Collins to advise her on the paper. She knew the week ahead would be a lot easier than the past one had been.

The bad news was that now Todd had come down with the flu, and that Mr. Collins was still expecting the students in his English class to hand in their essays the next day, flu or no flu.

"Poor Todd," Enid said as she and Elizabeth walked down the hallway together. "I just hope there are some good shows on television this week. I had nothing to watch but reruns of *I Love Lucy*." She made a face. "Last night I dreamed I was Ethel."

Elizabeth smiled. "Well, I'd rather be watching *I Love Lucy* than writing this essay for English."

Enid turned to her in surprise. "You mean you still haven't finished it? I thought it was due tomorrow."

Elizabeth's blue-green eyes darkened. "It is."

"That's not like you," Enid said. "You usually have your homework done days before it has to be in."

Elizabeth made a face. "Tell me about it. I was so busy trying to edit the paper . . ." She sighed. "It's not just that, though. The assignment is to compare something written with something visual. You know, to show how each uses imagery and symbols, and if they differ and why. I've chosen a poem and a painting with the same theme, but I can't seem to get my ideas together."

"*You* can't get your ideas together?" Enid put her hand on Elizabeth's forehead. "Maybe you're coming down with the flu, too," she teased.

"It's not the poem I'm having the problem with," Elizabeth explained. "It's the painting. I know I'm supposed to find all these thoughts and emotions in it, but to tell the truth, Enid, all I see is a picture."

Enid laughed. "I know what you mean." She lowered her voice melodramatically. "I've never really understood what the big deal is about the *Mona Lisa*. I mean, so she's smiling. So what?"

Elizabeth laughed.

"Why don't you ask Olivia for help?" Enid suggested. "She's brilliant at art and she's a good writer, too."

"I thought of that," Elizabeth said glumly. "But she's always so busy. I've hardly seen her at all except for Saturday night, and—I don't know, she was in a funny mood. I had the feeling she was upset about something, but I couldn't figure out what. She wasn't very friendly to me."

"It's probably just all the pressure she's under

78

right now," Enid said. "But you'd better ask someone," she went on. "Tomorrow's only twenty-four hours away."

Since Todd wasn't around, Elizabeth decided to spend her lunch hour in the *Oracle* office working on her English essay. She spread the pages of notes she had taken in front of her, staring down at them unhappily. "If only I'd paid attention the day Mr. Collins talked about symbols and imagination," she mumbled. "If only I was as good at art as I am at English."

"Do you always talk to yourself?" asked a voice behind her. "Or is it only when I'm around?"

Elizabeth turned to the door. "Rod! I didn't even hear you come in!"

"That's because you're so busy talking to yourself all the time." He held up a small brown paper bag. "Enid said you'd locked yourself away to work on your English essay, so I brought you something to keep your strength up." He sat on the edge of Elizabeth's desk and opened the bag. "Behold! Chocolate chip cookies."

"I was hoping you had some inspiration in that bag," Elizabeth said with a rueful smile.

"Don't knock chocolate chip cookies," Rod said, handing her one. "Legend has it that when William Shakespeare was writing *Macbeth*, he consumed over forty dozen chocolate chip cookies. Twenty dozen with nuts."

Elizabeth bit into the cookie, thinking how nice it was of Rod to come by to cheer her up. He was turning out to be a real friend. His presence made her feel calmer, just as it had the week before, when she had been in such a panic about the paper.

"Delicious," she said. "But I could still use some inspiration. I haven't started worrying about this week's *Oracle* yet because I don't even have a draft of my essay."

He looked down at the pages of notes as he munched a cookie. "What's wrong?" he asked, scattering crumbs across the desk. "You seem to have enough material there."

Elizabeth made a face. "The problem is that I don't know much about art," she said with a laugh. "I can write about how and why a poem works, but when it comes to a painting, I have no idea what to say."

"Well, you've come to the right person." He passed her another cookie. "Not only do I provide the best snacks in town, but it just so happens that I know a lot about painting."

Elizabeth stared at him. Of course. Why hadn't she thought of him before? Rod was one of the most talented artists in the school. "You really think you could help me get started?"

"Think?" He gave her a scornful look. "I don't *think*, I know I can. Why don't we meet at the Dairi Burger after school and toss some ideas around?"

Elizabeth looked down at her notes. Mr. Collins never objected to students brainstorming, and she was definitely in a bind. "That sounds great," she said, helping herself to another cookie. "I'm certainly glad you dropped by." She laughed. "You may have saved my life. Again."

*　　*　　*

"So then the vampire gives up and moves to Idaho and opens a gas station," Rod finished. He was sprawled in the seat across from Elizabeth, looking relaxed and happy. "It's a great movie."

"It sounds wild," Elizabeth said. "I didn't know you knew so much about films." In fact, she hadn't known he knew so much about music, television, sun poisoning, or tropical fish, either. But she was learning quickly. She and Rod had been in the Dairi Burger for an hour, and Rod had stopped talking only long enough to eat an order of fries and compliment her on her sweater.

"It's strange, isn't it?" Rod asked, suddenly becoming serious. "We've known each other for so long, but we've never really had a chance to talk like this before."

Elizabeth was beginning to wish that they *weren't* having a chance to talk like this now. As interesting and amusing as Rod was, work seemed to be the last thing on Rod's mind. No matter how hard she tried, the one thing she couldn't get him to talk about was her English essay. Instead, he joked and chatted about everything else under the sun, almost as if they were on a date. Almost as if he were trying to impress her.

"I guess it's lucky I needed help with this paper," she said, trying to sound lighthearted.

Rod nodded. "It sure is." He leaned toward her. "You know what I first noticed about you?" he asked, seeming as though he was already tired of discussing her paper.

Elizabeth made a valiant attempt to get him back on track. "That I knew nothing about art and was going to get an F in English because of it?"

He took her hand in his. "That you don't bite your nails. It drives me crazy when girls bite their nails. It's Olivia's only fault."

"If I don't get this essay done, I'm going to wind up biting my nails all the way down to my knuckles," Elizabeth said.

Rod laughed. "And the second thing I noticed was that you have a great sense of humor."

Elizabeth looked from Rod's smiling face to the hand holding hers, and began to feel really uncomfortable. *It's a good thing I have a great sense of humor*, she told herself. *Because I have the feeling I'm going to need it.*

"This was a terrific idea," DeeDee Gordon said to Olivia as they parked the car behind the Dairi Burger. "I'm starving."

"You're always starving," Olivia said, smiling at her friend.

"No, I'm not," argued DeeDee. "I'm always hungry, but this afternoon I'm starving."

Olivia followed DeeDee across the parking lot, thinking about the conversation she had had that afternoon with Rod. Monday was the day she and Rod usually stopped at the Dairi Burger after school just to hang out and talk. But when she had suggested it to him earlier that day, he'd said he couldn't make it because he had to give a friend a hand with an English assignment. When Olivia had laughed, he had looked at her defensively. "I don't see what's so funny. Some people think I'm pretty good at writing." If she hadn't been annoyed that he was missing their Monday afternoon date, she would have let his remark go. But she *was* annoyed, so she had made a rude comment and stormed off.

"Maybe I'll have onion rings *and* fries," DeeDee was saying as she followed Olivia through the door.

Olivia stopped so abruptly that DeeDee plowed into her.

"What's the matter?" asked DeeDee. "Aren't there any tables?"

Olivia's eyes were fixed on a spot at the far left corner of the restaurant, where Rod Sullivan and Elizabeth Wakefield sat at a small table, smiling into each other's eyes and holding hands. A tornado of emotion swept through Olivia. Rod and Elizabeth—she should have known! She *had* known! Some small part of her mind had tried to tell the rest of her that Rod's interest in Elizabeth wasn't platonic, but would she listen? No. And now this! Holding hands in the Dairi Burger, where everyone could see them, while she drove around Sweet Valley listening to DeeDee talk about food!

DeeDee gave her a nudge and said something about a space at the front, but Olivia wasn't listening. She was listening to the sound of laughter coming from the corner where her boyfriend was sitting. She couldn't remember when she had last seen Rod look so happy and relaxed. She clenched her jaw.

"Olivia," DeeDee said, "do you think we could sit down? I'm going to pass out from hunger in about two seconds."

Olivia bit her lip. He had said he was giving a friend a hand with an assignment. And to think that it hadn't even occurred to her that the "friend" he was talking about was Elizabeth, or that the "hand" he was giving her was the one that was wrapped around Elizabeth's own!

Olivia swung around suddenly, knocking DeeDee into a potted plant. "Come on," she ordered. "Let's get out of here."

DeeDee stared at her in total disbelief. "But what about my onion rings?"

Olivia grabbed DeeDee by the arm and yanked her through the door.

Finally realizing that Rod had no intention of removing his hand from hers, Elizabeth pulled away with so much force that she knocked over his water glass. Was it possible? Did Rod have some ulterior motive for offering to help her? Had all his helpfulness and friendliness lately meant that he secretly wanted to go out with her? Elizabeth watched him as he mopped up the spilled water with a wad of napkins. *It can't be*, she told herself. *It just can't. Rod's crazy about Olivia. They're one of the happiest couples I know. He's not interested in me.* The image of Olivia sitting across from her in that same room the other night came into Elizabeth's mind. Olivia, normally so funny and full of life, had looked unhappy and had hardly bothered to participate in the conversation. Why? Had she and Rod had a fight? Was there some trouble between them?

As though he felt her looking at him, Rod raised

his eyes to hers. "What's the matter?" he asked, instantly concerned. "You look really worried."

Elizabeth opened her mouth to speak. She should tell him what was on her mind—that was the right thing to do. But somehow she just couldn't. The expression on his face was so sincere and concerned. How could she doubt someone who had gone to so much trouble for her? She closed her mouth again. Suddenly she almost doubted her own motives in asking for his help.

Rod snapped his fingers. "I know what it is," he said. "It's that essay. Well, don't you worry, Elizabeth. I've been thinking about it all afternoon and I have quite a few ideas that I hope will help."

Relief rushed through her. Rod wasn't playing games with her; he had probably just been trying to put her at ease. Elizabeth reached for her notebook and pen. "OK," she said. "I'm ready."

Honesty really does make you feel good, Jessica thought as she walked up the Wakefields' driveway. That morning she had put her vow of honesty into action. She had told Amy she was wearing too much mascara. She had told Robin Wilson that her new cheer was as exciting as a glass of water. She had explained to Mr. Jaworski, her history teacher, that the real reason Kirk Anderson wasn't in class wasn't because of the flu, but because of the beach. When she had overheard John Pfeifer telling Artie Western how crazy Jennifer Mitchell was about him, she candidly explained to John that, in fact, she'd heard that Jennifer was thinking of breaking up with him.

Jessica skipped through the door. She felt like the child in the story about the emperor's new clothes. The child had been the only one with enough sense to tell the truth, and so was Jessica.

Prince Albert, the Wakefields' golden retriever, came out to greet her, his tail wagging furiously. Jessica patted his head. "You're getting fat, dog," she told him, continuing her policy of total honesty. "You're going to have to do something about that tummy."

Unlike Amy, who had gotten all offended and snotty when faced with the truth, Prince Albert licked her hand.

Mr. and Mrs. Wakefield were just getting their coats on when Jessica sailed into the living room.

"Oh, there you are," said Mrs. Wakefield. "I was just about to leave you a note." She pointed the pencil she was holding at Jessica. "There are leftovers in the fridge for you and Elizabeth to heat up for your supper, and I want you to remember that tonight's your night to take out the garbage."

Jessica studied her parents critically. They looked very dressed up for a Monday night. Her father was wearing his best gray suit, and her mother was wearing a beige silk dress Jessica had never seen before and her favorite pearl necklace. "Are you two going out or something?" she asked.

"We've got a big dinner with one of my firm's most important clients," Mr. Wakefield said, sounding pleased. He adjusted his tie.

Jessica turned back to her mother. "And *that's* what you're wearing?"

Mrs. Wakefield looked down at herself. "Well,

yes." She glanced at Mr. Wakefield, then back at her daughter. "What's wrong with it? Don't you like it?"

"You look like a graham cracker," Jessica announced bluntly. She shook her head. "No one wears beige in the evening, Mom. Especially not if they have your coloring."

Mrs. Wakefield opened her mouth, but no words came out.

"Jessica." Mr. Wakefield cleared his throat. "We all know what an authority on fashion you are, but I happen to think that your mother looks just . . . just fine in that dress."

Jessica rolled her eyes. "Well, you would, wouldn't you?" She pointed to the glass meerkats staring at them from the mantel. "I mean, anybody who would buy a monstrosity like that . . . you wouldn't notice if Mom were wearing a burlap sack."

As she sauntered toward the kitchen to get a snack—honesty making a girl feel hungry as well as free—Jessica heard her parents' voices.

"I thought you told me this dress looked terrific on me," Mrs. Wakefield hissed.

Mr. Wakefield's voice was loud and full of outrage. "And I thought *you* told *me* my meerkats were attractive and poignant."

After over an hour of driving around with DeeDee, trying to calm down, Olivia finally headed home. DeeDee had told her that she had overreacted and that she should have gone up to Rod right then and there and found out the truth.

"You're letting your imagination run away with you," DeeDee had said. "They were sitting in the Dairi Burger having a soda, Olivia, not sneaking around behind your back."

"But they were holding hands," Olivia had pointed out.

DeeDee had rolled her eyes. "Elizabeth Wakefield was sitting in the Dairi Burger holding hands with someone else's boyfriend? Have you lost your mind?"

Olivia marched into her house, banging the door behind her. Maybe DeeDee was right. Maybe she should have confronted Rod when she had the chance, instead of running out like a coward. Maybe she should have walked right up to his table and demanded to know what was going on.

Her eyes fell on the telephone in the hall. *Do it now*, she urged herself. *Just pick up the phone and call him.*

The voice on the Sullivans' answering machine told her that no one was home and asked her to leave a message after the tone. Olivia dropped the receiver back into its cradle with a clatter. *Now what?* she asked herself. *Wait till he gets back?* But she didn't want to wait. Olivia stared at the phone. Elizabeth wouldn't lie. If Rod really had been making a pass, Elizabeth would tell her.

Olivia took her address book out of her bag and dialed Elizabeth's number.

Elizabeth raced home from her meeting with Rod feeling hopeful and almost excited. Rod had given her some terrific ideas, and combined with the notes and jottings she already had, she knew she could shape them into a decent paper. Or she could as long as she did nothing else all night. She didn't have time to chat with Jessica, eat leftovers, or even scratch Prince Albert behind the ears.

Elizabeth was halfway through her first draft when Olivia called.

Her first thought was that Olivia must have read her poem on the Amazon already. "Hi, Olivia," she said, trying to sound casual. "What's up?"

She could tell Olivia was trying to sound casual, too. Elizabeth's heart sank. Olivia didn't like her poem after all.

Olivia laughed nervously. "Oh, nothing much," she said. "It's just that . . . well . . . I happened to see you and Rod in the Dairi Burger this afternoon, and I was wondering what was going on," she said quickly.

Elizabeth had been so sure that Olivia was going to tell her she didn't like her poem that she wasn't certain she'd heard her right. "What?"

Olivia took an audible breath. "It's just that Rod didn't say he was meeting you," she said. Elizabeth could hear the tension in her voice. "So, you know, I was wondering what you guys were doing there."

For a few seconds, Elizabeth couldn't answer. The doubts she had been feeling earlier about Rod's motives returned in a rush. Why hadn't Rod told Olivia he was meeting her? Was he trying to make a play for her? She wondered if she should have said something to him after all.

Olivia went on quickly. "I know you, Elizabeth. I mean, I'm not suggesting anything . . . I was just surprised, that's all."

Surprised. Olivia had said she was surprised—not worried, not suspicious. Elizabeth shoved the doubts away again. Nothing had happened. Nothing had even almost happened. Rod hadn't made a pass at her. He'd been friendly and helpful, but that was no crime. He probably just hadn't had a chance to tell Olivia he was meeting Elizabeth.

"Nothing was going on," Elizabeth said sincerely. "I was having trouble with my English essay, and Rod offered to help me at the last minute."

"I'm usually the one who helps him with his English assignments," Olivia said, but she sounded relieved.

Her relief was contagious. Although it struck Elizabeth as strange that someone who wrote as well as Rod needed help with English, she shoved that thought away, too. "Well, I guess this one was more up his alley than mine," Elizabeth said. She explained the assignment and how much trouble she was having with it. "I just couldn't think of how to write about the painting," Elizabeth said. "That's why I asked Rod for help."

Olivia cleared her throat. "This sounds a little crazy, but can I just ask what was he helping you with when he was holding your hand?"

"My hand?" Elizabeth repeated. She had almost managed to forget the anxious feeling she'd had when Rod wouldn't let go of her hand. Again she pushed it out of her mind, along with all the other things she didn't want to think about. "He wasn't really holding my hand," she said with a laugh. "He was just checking to see if I bit my nails."

"Oh," Olivia said, again sounding relieved. "He drives me crazy about my nails."

"He did say it was your only fault," Elizabeth said.

"He did? Rod said that?" Olivia laughed, but this time there wasn't any nervousness in it.

"Shower's free!"

Elizabeth opened her eyes. Where was she? What time was it? She looked toward the window. Sunlight was streaming through the curtains. *It can't be morning,* Elizabeth thought, desperately. She looked over at her desk. The lamp was still on. "Oh, no," she groaned. "I don't believe this!"

Everything came back to her. She had finally finished the draft of her essay at twelve-thirty. But she'd been so tired that when she tried to revise it, her eyes wouldn't stay open. The last thing she remembered was lying down on the bed for a short nap. *Just ten minutes,* she remembered telling herself. *Just ten minutes, and I'll be ready to go again.*

"Hey, sleepyhead!" Jessica called from the hallway. "You'd better get up or you're going to be late!"

Elizabeth jumped out of bed and snatched her essay off the desk. While she pulled clothes out of her dresser and closet, she read it through. It wasn't bad. It wasn't good, not *really* good. She hadn't really had a chance to digest the ideas Rod had given her and express them in her own way. But it wasn't bad, either. Mr. Collins would understand

91

that she had been under a lot of pressure with the newspaper. Just this once she could turn in something that wasn't up to her usual standards. But he would never understand if his star student didn't hand in anything.

Just this once . . . Elizabeth said to herself as she put the essay into her knapsack.

Seven

Jessica sat in history class watching a fly try to find
a way out the window. She wished she could find a
way out the window, too. Up at the front of the
room, Winston Egbert, Bruce Patman, Andrea
Slade, and Rosa Jameson were giving their group
talk on the French Revolution. Mr. Jaworski had di-
vided the class into groups of four and given each
group a topic to present. He seemed to think that
the class would be more interested in the topics and
get more out of them if they had to teach them
themselves.

Jessica yawned. Mr. Jaworski was wrong. It was
bad enough listening to him drone on and on about
dead kings and generals, but it was a lot better than
listening to Winston Egbert try to explain the
causes of the French Revolution. *It was a revolution
after all!* Jessica thought as Winston stumbled

through his speech. *It must have been more exciting than this!*

Josh Brown, sitting two seats away, caught her eye and pretended to be dropping off to sleep. Jessica pointed to the girl next to her, who was practically snoring. She glanced around the room. While Mr. Jaworski sat in the front row looking interested and attentive, people doodled in their notebooks, a few were writing letters, and Aaron Dallas and April Dawson were playing tic-tac-toe. Jessica turned back to the window. The fly was gone. She yawned again.

After what seemed like hours, if not days, Mr. Jaworski stood up and thanked Winston, Andrea, Bruce, and Rosa for their talk.

"All right," he said to the rest of the class. "Let's have your comments on the presentation."

One or two hands went up. April Dawson said she thought the talk was very interesting. John Pfeifer said that he thought it was very interesting, too, but that Rosa could have spoken a little louder. Aaron said he thought he had learned a lot. Josh said he really thought he understood the French Revolution now. Jessica shifted restlessly in her seat. No one ever said anything critical or unkind about the presentations—anything honest. Even though it was obvious that everyone had been as bored by the talks as Jessica was, they always pretended that they had been spellbound through the whole thing. *Talk about dishonesty*, thought Jessica. *George Washington would be horrified!*

Mr. Jaworski nodded at her. "Yes, Jessica? Would you like to give us your opinion?"

Jessica raised her head. The old, dishonest Jessica would have told Mr. Jaworski that she thought the presentation was great. But the truth had set her free. She smiled. "Yes," she said in a strong, clear voice. "I would."

No sooner had the bell rung than Bruce, Winston, Andrea, and Rosa all rushed over to Jessica's desk, murder in their eyes. Jessica looked at the four angry faces surrounding her. They all started shouting at once.

"Thanks a lot!" Andrea snapped. "Remind me not to count on you for anything again as long as I live."

" 'Superficial and monotonous'!" Bruce said with a disgusted face. "How could you say that I was superficial and monotonous, Jessica? Me!"

"That's better than being told that you're the best cure for insomnia since counting sheep," Rosa said sourly.

Winston shook his head. "I don't get it, Jessica. Why would you want to embarrass us like that?"

Jessica stood up. "I don't understand why you're all so upset," she said calmly. "Mr. Jaworski asked me for my opinion, and that's what I gave. You wouldn't want me to lie, would you?"

"No one's asking you to lie," Rosa said. "But you didn't have to tear us apart."

Winston nodded. "You could have stressed our good points instead of picking on our weaknesses. That's what everybody else did."

Jessica stared back. Somehow she doubted that this was the right moment to tell him she didn't think their presentation had had any good points.

"You embarrassed us," Andrea complained.

"But I wasn't trying to embarrass you," Jessica said reasonably. "I was telling you what I really thought."

Andrea scowled. "You think I'm boring?"

Winston flapped his arms in the air. "You think I could make Disneyland sound dull?"

Jessica looked from one to another. "Well, yes," she said. "Actually I do."

Rosa put her hands on her hips. "And if you were grading us, you would have given us a D?"

"Around a D, yes."

"We're trying to pass this class, Jessica," Andrea said evenly. "We don't need you telling Mr. Jaworski he should give us a D."

Jessica frowned. "But what was I supposed to say? That's what I thought."

Bruce thumped his fist on her desk. "Well, then, how come you're the only one who thought so?" he demanded. "Everyone else seemed to think we should get at least a B."

Jessica picked up her books. "That's because everyone else was lying."

Mr. Collins had asked to see Elizabeth in his classroom after school on Wednesday. Elizabeth hoped that whatever he had to say wasn't going to take too long, because she still had to put the paper to bed. This week hadn't been half as hectic as the last one, but she still had work to do.

It can't be anything too important, she told herself as she hurried down the hall to the English room.

He probably just wants to tell me how much he liked last Friday's Oracle *or something.*

Mr. Collins was sitting at his desk, his head resting on one hand, staring down at a paper in front of him, when Elizabeth entered the room. She couldn't help noticing how worried and tired he looked. *He must still be suffering from the after-effects of the flu,* she decided.

"Mr. Collins?" she called softly. "You wanted to see me?"

He looked up at the sound of her voice. "Yes, Elizabeth," he said quietly. He got to his feet.

Elizabeth stopped in the doorway, suddenly feeling uneasy. Mr. Collins was one of her favorite teachers and a good friend. Yet the look he was giving her was distant and guarded. "Mr. Collins, is something wrong?"

He nodded. "Perhaps you'd better shut the door," he said in a serious, formal voice she had almost never heard him use with her before.

Elizabeth's uneasiness increased. She obediently closed the door behind her.

"What is it?" she asked, walking over to the desk.

Mr. Collins picked up the paper he had been staring at when she came in and handed it to her.

Elizabeth glanced at the pages she was holding, totally bewildered. The essay Mr. Collins had given her was covered with comments in red ink and there was a heavily written F at the top. Why was Mr. Collins giving her someone else's English essay to look at? She didn't want to know who had failed.

His eyes bored into hers. "Well?"

Elizabeth looked more closely at the paper in her hand. Her mouth opened in stunned disbelief. It wasn't someone else's essay she was holding, it was *hers!* But it couldn't be hers. She knew that this last paper hadn't been her best, but it couldn't have been bad enough to get an F. She stared at the name in the upper right-hand corner: Elizabeth Wakefield.

"I'd like an explanation," Mr. Collins said simply.

Elizabeth raised her eyes. "An explanation? An explanation of what?"

Mr. Collins took the essay from her hand. "For this!" he said, holding it in front of her.

"Well . . ." Elizabeth took a deep breath. She could understand that Mr. Collins was disappointed in her, but he seemed to be taking her poor performance personally. "I know it's not the best I could do," she began, "but I was so busy with the newspaper last week because everyone was out sick that I just couldn't get started on it, and then I fell asleep while I was trying to revise it, and—"

"Elizabeth!" Mr. Collins cut her off. "Please don't make this any harder than it already is. I spent a sleepless night trying to come up with reasons why you would do this, trying to explain it to myself somehow." There was real pain in his eyes when he looked at her. "You're the last person in the world I would have thought would do something like this."

Suddenly Elizabeth realized that she and Mr. Collins weren't talking about the same thing. The anger and disappointment in his face weren't about her essay not being up to her usual standards. It was something else. Something really awful. "Do something like what?" she asked uncertainly.

Mr. Collins just stared at her for a second. "Plagiarize the work of Archie Fox, the country's best-known art critic," he said. He ran a hand through his hair and sighed.

Elizabeth tried to make some sense of what she was hearing. Mr. Collins was accusing her of plagiarism, saying that her essay wasn't her own work, that it was the work of some man she had never even heard of. "Me?" she repeated. "You're saying that I—"

Mr. Collins cut her off again. He pointed to her name on the top of the page. "You are Elizabeth Wakefield, aren't you?"

Elizabeth nodded.

"And you did write an essay comparing a poem on childhood with a painting of three children playing ball, didn't you?"

"Yes," Elizabeth mumbled. "I did, but—"

Mr. Collins sighed again. "There's nothing wrong with using and paraphrasing someone else's ideas, Elizabeth. But you know you must credit the source. To take whole chunks from *Art and Film* and present them as though they were your own . . ." He dropped the paper on the desk. "Did you think I'd give you an assignment like this and not have read the most recent theories myself?"

Elizabeth wished desperately that she could think of something to say. But she had no excuse. The paragraphs Mr. Collins had circled in red were the ones Rod had given her in the Dairi Burger. He must have gotten them from Archie Fox's book and not bothered to mention that to her.

The room was spinning. Elizabeth was speechless with shame and confusion. *What have I done?* she asked herself. She and Mr. Collins had always had a relationship built on mutual respect. But now as she looked at him all she saw in his eyes was disappointment.

He cleared his throat. "Elizabeth," he said gently, "I know this isn't like you. I know you've been under a lot of pressure in the last week, and I wish I'd been here to help you. But that still isn't an excuse. If you could just give me some idea . . ." He held out his hands. "If you're having some trouble at home, or with Todd . . ."

Elizabeth shook her head. "No," she said in a choked whisper. "No, I'm not having any trouble." She couldn't even blame Rod. She was angry with him—angry and bewildered that he hadn't told her where his ideas had come from—but she still couldn't blame him. The truth was that she was just as guilty of stealing his ideas as he was of stealing those of Archie Fox. She had known she shouldn't just put down what he'd told her as though she had thought of it herself, but she had done it anyway. Being tired no longer seemed like much of an excuse.

"Plagiarism is a very serious offense," Mr. Collins said sadly. "If you were the professional writer you want to be someday, your whole career could be ruined by something like this."

Elizabeth choked back the hot tears that were threatening to fill her eyes.

Mr. Collins sat on the edge of the desk, his hands folded on his lap. "Without some help from you, I can't try to defend you. Considering how serious this is, I'm going to have to give you an F on the paper. This puts your quarter English grade in real jeopardy. You know the rules about grades and extracurricular activities. I have no choice but to suspend you from the newspaper for the time being."

"What?"

"You heard me, Elizabeth. Unless you can come up with some reasonable explanation for what you did, I'll have to fail you on this essay. *The Oracle* is going to have to do without you."

Elizabeth stood in shock. She was off the paper! The Oracle had been such a large and important part of her life for so long that she couldn't conceive of not being a part of it. Off the newspaper! Stunned, and fighting hard not to burst into tears, Elizabeth left the classroom without another word.

Right outside the door, she walked into Olivia.

The smile of greeting froze on Olivia's face. "Elizabeth!" she cried. "What happened? Are you all right?"

The kindness in Olivia's voice caused a single tear to slide down Elizabeth's cheek. Her first instinct was just to let go and tell Olivia everything that had happened.

"Elizabeth?" Olivia asked, her voice gentle with concern. "Elizabeth, what's wrong?"

Elizabeth knew she couldn't tell her the truth any more than she had been able to tell Mr. Collins. Olivia was Rod's girlfriend. How could Elizabeth tell her about the plagiarism charges without involving Rod?

Somehow, Elizabeth managed to speak. The voice that came out of her mouth was not her normal, confident voice, but at least it was forming words. "I'm OK," she said. "Really. Thanks, but I've got to go now." She could feel Olivia's worried eyes on her back as she hurried down the hall.

"Have you talked to Elizabeth since you went with her to the Dairi Burger?" Olivia asked Rod as they walked across the parking lot to his car after school.

After her telephone conversation with Elizabeth the previous afternoon, Olivia had finally gotten through to Rod. She had told him that she'd seen him with Elizabeth, and how upset it had made her. Rod had laughed at her concern. How many times did he have to tell her that he wasn't interested in anybody else? he had asked. And if he were, why would he take her someplace where everyone would see them? And why would it be Elizabeth, whose relationship with Todd was so strong that people assumed they were practically married?

Now Rod shook his head. "I've seen her in class, but I haven't really talked to her. Why? Is something wrong?"

Olivia told him about running into Elizabeth outside of Mr. Collins's classroom. "Maybe it was nothing," she said, "but she looked so miserable that it really worried me."

Rod put his arm around Olivia's shoulder. "You worry

too much, that's your problem. I'm sure it was nothing. Maybe it's some problem with *The Oracle*. You know how seriously Elizabeth takes everything." He gave her a squeeze. "Just like you."

Olivia laughed. "Yeah, I'm sure you're right," she said as they reached the car. "It was probably nothing."

"Why is Andrea Slade looking at you like that?" Lila asked as she, Jessica, and Amy slid into a booth at the Dairi Burger. "If looks could kill, you'd be in intensive care by now."

Jessica glanced over at Andrea. "We had a little argument in history today," Jessica confessed.

"You argued about history?" Amy said. "How can you argue about history? It's been over for years."

"No, not *about* history," Jessica said. She told them about Mr. Jaworski and the class presentation, and how she had made the only honest comments in the class.

"Some people really are too much," Lila said when Jessica had finished. "I mean, you were obviously in the right, Jess. If Mr. Jaworski wants to know what you thought, you should tell him the truth."

Amy nodded. "I agree. And who knows? In years to come, they might all thank you for being so honest. Because of what you told them, Winston might someday get a job as a television announcer, or Rosa might go in for public speaking. You probably did them a big favor."

"I knew you two would understand," Jessica

said contentedly. "When they were all giving me such a hard time after class, I felt like telling them to grow up. I felt like saying, 'Do you think Lila would act like this if I told her that no one ever understands a word she says when she gives a speech because she talks so fast?'"

Lila looked up from pouring ketchup on her fries. "What?"

Jessica tossed her hair over her shoulder. "Really, why should it be so horrible to learn the truth about yourself?" She turned to Amy. "You know that everyone laughs at the way you run when we play softball, but you don't mind, do you?"

Amy put her glass on the table with a smack. "*Who* laughs at me?"

Jessica's smile became a little less bright. Both Amy and Lila were looking at her in very much the same way that Andrea had been looking at her only a few minutes before. "But you know that," she said, her eyes moving from one to the other. "Everybody knows. That's why they call Lila Speedo and you Clodhopper."

Amy edged away from Jessica and folded her arms across her chest. "They call *me* Clodhopper?"

Lila stabbed a french fry. "They call *me* Speedo?"

Jessica nodded. "I thought you both knew that."

"And what do they call you?" Lila asked, as sweet as strychnine. "Little Big Mouth?"

Elizabeth was relieved to find the house empty when she got home. She went straight to her room and threw herself on the bed. The tears she had

104

been holding back exploded. Elizabeth let them come. She cried so much and for so long that, in the end, she must have fallen asleep. When she woke up, the sun was almost setting, and Jessica was staring down at her.

"I called and called," Jessica said. "Why are you sleeping? Are you coming down with the flu?"

Elizabeth sat up, rubbing her eyes. "No," she said. "I'm fine."

"Ugh!" Jessica made a horrified face. "You may feel fine," she said, "but you look awful. Are you sure you're not sick? Your eyes are all red and puffy."

"Sit down," Elizabeth told her sister. "I have to tell you what happened."

Jessica listened to the whole story with a look of furious indignation on her face. "I don't believe this!" she raged when Elizabeth was done. "How could anyone accuse *you* of plagiarism? I've never heard anything so ridiculous in my entire life!"

"You can't blame Mr. Collins," Elizabeth said. "What else could he believe? He saw the evidence with his own eyes." She shrugged. "And anyway, it's true. I did use someone else's ideas."

Jessica's blue eyes blazed. "But you didn't do it purposely." She gave her sister a stern look. "I think you should have told Mr. Collins the truth. Maybe you did repeat everything Rod told you, and maybe that's wrong, but it's still not the same as deliberately stealing ideas from a published work. Rod should take some of the blame for this. He's the one who started it. He knew he was giving you this other guy's ideas."

105

"I couldn't do that," Elizabeth said. "I can't just turn Rod in."

Elizabeth knew that the old, not-quite-so-honest Jessica would have come up with at least three different schemes for getting even with Rod. And she also knew that the old Jessica would rather have dyed her hair mousy brown than tell on someone else. But the new Jessica seemed to view things more simply.

"So what?" Jessica demanded. "Rod's the one who got you into this. He deserves what he gets."

Elizabeth rested her chin in her hands. "I just wish I knew why he did it."

"You really are too much, you know that?" Jessica rolled her eyes. "Why do you think he did it? Obviously, he wanted to impress you."

Elizabeth looked at her sister sharply. No matter how much she might joke about Jessica's flirtatiousness, the fact was that Jessica was the local expert on boys. If Jessica thought Rod had done this because he was trying to impress her, then maybe Elizabeth's suspicions in the Dairi Burger the other day had been right. "I'm not sure," she said cautiously.

Jessica made another face. "Wake up, Liz. Rod has a crush on you. He didn't tell you all that stuff to get you in trouble, he told you all that stuff because he wanted you to like him."

"Do you really think so?"

"Of course I do. It couldn't be more obvious if he announced it on television."

Elizabeth had thought she couldn't feel any guiltier, but somehow she did. "But this is even worse," she groaned. "It means that not only am I guilty of plagiarism, I'm also guilty of encouraging Olivia's boyfriend."

Jessica shook her head. "He didn't need much encouragement, if you ask me. I've seen the way he looks at you, Liz. And if anybody looked at me like that, Sam would run him over with his dirt bike."

Elizabeth threw herself down on the bed and buried her face in her pillow. "What am I going to do?" she wailed. "This is the most awful mess I've ever been in."

"Tell Olivia exactly what happened," Jessica advised. "I guarantee she'll thank you for telling her the truth."

Eight

After a fitful night's sleep, Elizabeth woke up on Thursday morning knowing exactly what she had to do. Before she said anything to Olivia, she had to talk to Rod. She would tell him what had happened with Mr. Collins, and ask him straight out why he had misled her like that. She would ask him to go with her to Mr. Collins and explain the situation.

"You want me to go with you?" Jessica asked as they climbed out of the Jeep in the school parking lot.

Elizabeth gave her sister a weak smile. "No, thanks. I think this is something I have to do myself."

Jessica gave her a thumbs-up sign. "Just tell him that if he gives you any more trouble, he'll have to deal with me."

Elizabeth laughed in spite of herself. "I just want

to straighten everything out, not scare him to death," she said.

"Do you think we could go to the *Oracle* office and talk for a few minutes?" Elizabeth asked Rod when she ran into him by his locker.

"Sure," he said. "Your wish is my command."

Then I wish none of this had ever happened, Elizabeth thought as she led the way down the hall.

As soon as the office door shut behind them, Elizabeth told Rod about her talk with Mr. Collins as simply and unemotionally as she could. Rod listened to her with a blank expression on his face.

"I don't understand," he said when she had finished. "Why are you telling me all this?"

"Why?" Elizabeth stared at him in disbelief. "Because I'm trying to understand why you did this to me."

Rod shook his head. "Did what to you, Elizabeth? All I did was try to help out a friend. I never told you to use Archie Fox's ideas as though they were yours."

"But you didn't tell me they were *his* ideas, either," Elizabeth said. "You let me believe that they were yours."

Rod shrugged, but his expression was uneasy. "To tell you the truth, Elizabeth, his ideas and my ideas are all mixed together in my head. And anyway, I was just trying to give you something to get started with. You can't blame me for this."

"But you misled me," Elizabeth protested. "You went out of your way to make me trust you. You—"

"I tried to help you, Elizabeth, that's all." He

picked up his books and started toward the door. "Since when is friendship against the law?"

Jessica landed at the table where Lila, Claire Middleton, and Maria Santelli sat eating lunch. "Have you seen the poster outside the office?" she asked.

Lila looked up. "You mean Olivia Davidson's poster? The one asking for contributions to some weird issue of *Visions?*" She eyed Jessica quizzically. "Don't tell me you've decided to become the poet representative for endangered species as well as Sweet Valley's very own George Washington."

Jessica decided to ignore the dig. "No, not *that* poster. The one about the tryouts for the new choral group."

"A choral group?" Maria looked interested. "Sounds like fun."

"Well, that leaves me out," Claire said with a grin. "My voice is better suited for calling plays than singing. I think I'll stick to football."

"I think maybe I'll try out," Maria said.

"You?" Jessica turned to her in surprise. "But you can't sing, Maria. You're practically tone-deaf."

Maria dropped her fork. "No, I'm not. I used to be in the middle-school chorus. *And* I was in the variety show."

Jessica raised one eyebrow. "Exactly. With everyone else singing, no one in the audience could tell that you were in a different key. But I know for a fact that everyone used to call you One-note Santelli behind your back."

Claire and Lila started to giggle. Maria stood up,

shoving her chair back so roughly that it crashed to the floor. "That's it!" she snapped. "I've just about had it with you, Jessica Wakefield. You do nothing but go around insulting everyone. Who do you think you are, telling me that *I* can't sing? I sing just fine, for your information. I sing just great." She picked up her tray. "And now if you'll excuse me, I think I'll go sit somewhere else." She gave Jessica an icy look. "Somewhere where I won't be insulted."

Jessica watched her stomp off. "What's with her?" She turned to Claire. "Her temper is almost as bad as yours."

Tiny frown lines appeared on Claire's forehead. "As whose?" she asked cautiously.

"As yours," Jessica repeated. "Everybody still talks about the time you stormed out of class just because Ms. Ford got your name wrong."

Claire's sandwich fell to the table. "It wasn't because she got my—"

But Jessica wasn't listening to Claire's explanation. She was laughing at something that had obviously amused her. "Then how about that fight you had with Scott Trost?" Jessica rolled her eyes. "Whew. Talk about temper! You should have heard what he said afterward."

Claire's temper was beginning to make an appearance. Her eyes were blazing. "And what exactly *did* Scott say?"

"Jessica . . ." Lila said in a warning voice. "Maybe you should change the subject. That fight happened a long time ago. I'm sure Claire doesn't—"

"No," snapped Claire. "I want to hear what Scott said." She smiled bleakly. "After all, it's so refreshing to be told the truth, isn't it?"

Jessica smiled. At least Claire had the right attitude. Maria Santelli might not want to hear about her singing. Lila and Amy might get a little huffy when she pointed out something about them that they had been unaware of. But a lot of people, Jessica had discovered, actively sought the truth. Now that everyone knew that she always gave an honest answer, she found that she was constantly being bombarded with questions. *What did so-and-so really say about me? Did X really break up with Y? Do you think B really will call me? Did A say anything about me behind my back? Do you really think I need to lose weight?*

"You have no idea how many people have told me that," Jessica said.

Lila gave her a disgruntled look. "They were probably lying."

"What are you talking about, Lila?" Jessica asked. "You're the one who kept telling me that honesty is the best policy. You're the one who gave me that great magazine article."

"I know I did," Lila said. "But I think there's a difference between telling someone every awful thing people have said about them and telling them the truth."

"Well, I don't," Claire said in a tight voice. "And I want to hear every word that came out of Scott Trost's big, egotistical mouth."

Lila shook her head sadly as Jessica launched into a detailed account of Scott's version of his argument with Claire. "I feel like I've created a monster," she said.

Mr. Collins rapped on the table. "Before we start our meeting, I have an announcement to make that will affect all of you."

Olivia looked at the other *Oracle* staff members. They all looked as puzzled as she felt.

"What is it?" John Pfeifer joked. "Is Penny staying in Washington after all?"

Mr. Collins didn't smile. "Not quite," he said. "Penny will be back this weekend. The announcement is that Elizabeth Wakefield is temporarily off the paper. Effective immediately."

A stunned silence came over the room. Olivia couldn't believe her ears. She looked over at Rod. He was staring at Mr. Collins in obvious surprise.

Jennifer Mitchell laughed in disbelief. "Elizabeth not on the paper? You're kidding, right?"

Olivia could tell from Mr. Collins's face that he was not kidding. What could possibly have happened? she wondered.

"But why?" Tina Ayala asked. She looked at the rest of the staff with a nervous smile. "Elizabeth would never quit *The Oracle*. She loves this paper. And she's the best reporter we have."

Mr. Collins rapped for attention again. "I think perhaps we should call our meeting to order," he said stiffly.

Olivia remembered the look on Elizabeth's face when she had come out of Mr. Collins's classroom the afternoon before. This must have been what she was so upset about. Had Elizabeth been kicked off the paper?

"Hey, Olivia, the meeting's starting."

Olivia shook off her confused thoughts to find Rod leaning toward her. "I can't believe this," she whispered.

"It's probably nothing," Rod whispered back. "Mr. Collins did say it was temporary. It's probably just some little misunderstanding."

"Do you really think so?"

He nodded. "Sure. But in the meantime, if we mortals are going to put out a paper without our ace reporter, we're definitely going to need your help, you know."

The fact that the paper needed *her* made Elizabeth's problems fade a little from Olivia's mind. "Don't worry about that," she said. "You know you can count on me."

Elizabeth sat in the library until she was sure the *Oracle* staff meeting would be over. She wanted to get all her things out of the newspaper office right away. The sooner the better, she had decided. She didn't want to think of her notebooks and pens sitting in her desk, waiting for her. She didn't want any trace of herself left behind. Once she had everything out of there, it would really be over, and she could start thinking about what she was going to do with her life now that she wasn't going to be a writer after all.

Concentrating on what she had to do, Elizabeth marched down the hallway with a purposeful step.

She wanted to get in and out as quickly as possible or she might start crying again.

At the door to the office she paused for a second. This would be the last time she ever went in there. She took a deep breath and pushed open the door. *Just get it over with*, she ordered herself.

Elizabeth stood in the doorway. Not only could she hear her heart pounding, she could feel the blood rushing through her. She had been wrong. The staff meeting wasn't over. It was only just ending.

Mr. Collins looked up, his face ready to smile a greeting. Seeing who it was, however, his expression turned to embarrassment, and he quickly looked away and began fumbling with some papers on his desk.

Part of Elizabeth wanted to bolt through the door. *Don't be ridiculous*, she told herself. *Just act normally. These are your friends. Just act like nothing's wrong.*

Holding her head high, and hoping she was hiding the anxiety that was churning inside her, Elizabeth forced herself to walk over to her desk. But nothing was normal. She knew that. Swallowing hard, Elizabeth began quietly opening drawers and putting her things into her bag.

Mr. Collins finished handing out the assignments for the next issue. A dagger of unhappiness stabbed Elizabeth's heart. She should be sitting with everyone else, talking and joking about deadlines and problems. She glanced over at her coworkers. These were the people she had laughed with and worried with over dozens of issues.

116

These were the people she had argued with over cutting a story, changing a layout, or ordering pepperoni instead of mushroom pizza. Now they looked embarrassed, uncomfortable, unsure of what to say. John Pfeifer was trying to make his pen work. Jennifer Mitchell was searching for something in her backpack. Rod was getting his things together. Only Olivia met her eyes.

She wished she could explain to them all exactly what had happened.

Mr. Collins's voice boomed across the room. "That's it," he said. "I can't wait to read tomorrow's issue."

Elizabeth dropped the last pen into her bag. She might never read another issue of *The Oracle* again.

Olivia got to her feet as soon as the meeting was over. "Poor Elizabeth!" she said to Rod. "Why is everyone acting so strangely toward her?"

Rod looked uncomfortable. "I think everyone's just embarrassed. For her as much as for themselves." He lowered his voice. "And besides, Liv, maybe it'd just be better to, you know, not get involved right now. We don't know what happened. Maybe we should just wait till things blow over. Meddling isn't going to help Elizabeth or anybody else."

Olivia took a step away from him. She couldn't figure out what was wrong with Rod. Not only did he look uneasy, but here he was, the president of the Elizabeth Wakefield fan club, acting as though they shouldn't stand up for her. As though they should ignore her until things cooled down. "What are you talking about, 'not get involved'?" she demanded. "I thought Elizabeth was your friend."

He put a hand on her arm. "She is my friend, Olivia, but you have to be realistic—"

Olivia shook him off. Without another word she ran toward the parking lot to catch up with Elizabeth.

"I'm really glad you suggested going for a soda," Elizabeth said as she and Olivia sat down at a corner table in Casey's Place. "There's something I need to talk to you about."

Olivia nodded, taking in the strained look on Elizabeth's face and the unshed tears that glistened in her eyes.

"I never thought Jessica would be telling *me* that honesty is the best policy," Elizabeth said haltingly. "But I think this time my sister might be right. I feel like I should tell you what happened, right from the beginning."

Olivia had never seen Elizabeth in a state like this. "You can trust me," she promised. "I won't even tell Rod if you don't want me to."

When Elizabeth finished her story, Olivia sat back, sighed, and ran her hand through her hair. Of all the possible reasons for Elizabeth having to leave *The Oracle*, plagiarism would never have occurred to Olivia.

"Plagiarism?" she repeated. "But there must be some mistake. You're one of the most honest people I know. You're not a plagiarist!"

Elizabeth took another napkin from the holder

and wiped her eyes. "Not intentionally," she sniffled. "It was all because I was so busy with the newspaper, and I'd had so much trouble with the essay. Then Rod offered to help me with my English paper . . ."

A damp chill ran up Olivia's spine. "Rod?" she asked in a quiet voice. "What does he have to do with this?"

Painfully and haltingly, Elizabeth explained what had happened, as far as she understood it. "I know I'm not innocent," she concluded. "I didn't think to question what Rod told me, and I did put his ideas in my essay as though they were my own. But I never—I didn't think—" Fresh tears came to her eyes. "I just can't understand why he would do something like this to me. It's so unlike him."

All the while Elizabeth talked, Olivia had not said one word. She wasn't sure she could speak, and even if she could, she didn't know what to say. It felt as though the world had started spinning around her. Dozens of different thoughts and feelings stampeded through her—the worry that Rod was interested in Elizabeth, the jealousy she had felt, the lack of confidence in herself . . . The one thing she felt sure of was that Elizabeth was right about Rod. Getting anyone into trouble like this wasn't like him. He had his faults, she wouldn't deny that, but he wasn't mean or spiteful. There was, in fact, only one reason Rod would do something like this to Elizabeth: because he hadn't meant to. Because what he'd wanted to do was impress her, because he wanted her to like him as

119

much as he liked her. Olivia stared down at her hands. But Rod had denied that he was interested in Elizabeth. He'd promised her . . .

"Olivia, say something."

Olivia looked up. "I can't," she said in a hoarse whisper. "I don't understand why you're telling me all this. I don't understand what you want me to do."

"I want you to talk to Rod," Elizabeth said.

The image of Rod and Elizabeth sitting across from each other at the Dairi Burger, their hands entwined, drifted through Olivia's mind. Had Elizabeth told her the truth about what was going on that day? Had Rod? "Why don't you talk to him yourself?" Olivia asked, her tone sharper than she had intended. "You've had no trouble talking to him before."

"But I did talk to him," Elizabeth explained. "I spoke to him this morning. He says he hasn't done anything wrong."

"So?"

Elizabeth leaned toward Olivia. "I haven't said anything to Mr. Collins about what really happened, and I won't. I think it's up to Rod to tell the truth. I take full responsibility for what I've done wrong, but Rod has to take some responsibility, too."

"*If* he did anything wrong," Olivia said.

"You mean you don't believe me?"

Olivia pushed back her chair. "I mean I don't know what to believe." Suddenly all she wanted to do was get out of Casey's as fast as she could. "I'm sorry, Elizabeth. I know this is awful for you, but I don't know what to do." She picked up her bag and hugged it to her chest. "I just can't believe that Rod . . ."

"I can't believe that Rod would do this, either," Elizabeth said. "I'm sure he didn't mean for this to happen—" she began.

But Olivia cut her off. "I really am sorry," she said quickly, "but I have to go home now." She rushed out of Casey's without looking back.

"So much for honesty," said Elizabeth into the receiver.

"Even if Rod and Olivia don't want to hear the truth, Jessica's right—you did the best thing," Todd said. He sighed. "I just wish you'd told me last night what happened."

"I was going to, but I was so exhausted by the whole thing that after I talked to Jessica, all I wanted to do was go to sleep." She didn't bother adding that she hadn't really intended to tell him now, that she had wanted to wait until they were face to face. But she had been so upset when she got home from Casey's Place that she knew she had to talk to Todd. Even just asking whether he was feeling better would make her feel that the world wasn't as upside down as it seemed. But the sound of his voice, so normal and so full of affection, had started her crying again, and the next thing she knew the whole story had come out in a rush.

"It's going to be OK," he said soothingly. "The only thing you're really guilty of is an error in judgment. I'm sure Mr. Collins will realize that sooner or later."

Elizabeth blew her nose. "Not if Rod doesn't

come clean, he won't." She sighed. "What a mess I've made of everything. Rod's going on as though nothing's happened, Olivia isn't speaking to me, and my whole career is ruined. I'll never be a writer now. I'll never be anything."

"Hello?" Todd shouted. "Hello? I was talking to Elizabeth Wakefield, but something's wrong with the line. Hello?"

"I'm here!" Elizabeth shouted back. "Can't you hear me?"

"But you can't be Elizabeth Wakefield. Elizabeth would never give up so easily."

Elizabeth smiled through her tears. And then she began to laugh.

By the time Olivia reached home that afternoon, she knew what she had to do. She marched into the house, up the stairs, and into her room. She dumped her things on the bed and picked up the phone. She had to talk to Rod. She had to hear his version of what had happened—and why.

Rod's response was immediate. "You know what happened, Olivia. I haven't been keeping any secrets from you. I gave Elizabeth some help with her English essay, that's all. How was I supposed to know she'd just take everything I told her and use it as her own?"

"But . . ." Olivia wasn't sure what to say. The real question she wanted to ask was, why? Why had he gone to so much trouble for Elizabeth? Why was he so full of her praises before and so cool about her now?

"But what, Liv? All I did was try to help a friend."

Olivia took a deep breath. "You're sure of that, Rod? You're sure you didn't have any other feelings for Elizabeth but friendship?"

"Yes," Rod said, his voice hard with indignation. "For the last time, Olivia, I'm sure."

Nine

Standing on the Davidsons' front porch, Rod put his arms around Olivia and kissed her good night. It was a long, tender kiss, and Olivia could feel her heart pounding. She leaned her head on his shoulder and they stood there for a few minutes, their arms around each other. Suddenly the hall light went on.

"Uh-oh," Olivia said softly. "I think my mother wants me inside."

Rod kissed the tip of her nose. "Sweet dreams," he whispered. "I'll call you in the morning."

"I'll be waiting," she whispered back.

"Did you have a nice time, sweetie?" her mother asked as Olivia entered the house.

"Very nice," Olivia said as she floated up the stairs. *Nice* hardly described it. *Fantastic, awesome, spectacular*—none of those words really described the evening Olivia had just had.

Rod had taken her to a candlelit dinner at the Box Tree Café. He had brought her flowers. He had been attentive and romantic all through the meal. And afterward, as they held hands across the table, smiling at each other in the flickering light, he had presented her with a pair of silver earrings shaped like stars. "Something unusual for someone unusual," he had said, squeezing her hand. After dinner, they had taken a walk along the beach beneath a full yellow moon.

Feeling as though she were walking on clouds, Olivia got ready for bed.

Not only had she and Rod had the best date in the history of the world, but she, Olivia Davidson, had had one of the best days of her entire life. First thing that morning, Mr. Collins had bumped into her in the hallway and asked her to meet him in the *Oracle* office right after lunch. Olivia was half afraid that he wanted to talk to her about Elizabeth, but he hadn't. He had wanted to talk to her about her. He'd asked her to help him with the editorial work until Penny had a chance to settle back into things.

Olivia slipped under the covers, gazing up at the moonlight streaming across the ceiling, reliving every detail of her wonderful day. Suddenly, unbidden, Elizabeth entered her thoughts. Elizabeth racing out of Mr. Collins's room the other afternoon. Elizabeth sitting across from her at Casey's, wiping away the tears with paper napkins. Olivia closed her eyes. *There's nothing I can do to help Elizabeth,* she told herself. *Rod's as innocent in all this as she is. What could I do?*

* * *

126

Saturday was Jessica's lazy day—or, as her family often joked, her lazier day—and she liked to sleep as late as she wanted. Elizabeth always got up early and was usually out of the house before Jessica was out of her pajamas.

That Saturday morning, Jessica woke up even later than usual. She groaned. Elizabeth had probably written fifteen poems about rare Amazonian snakes by now. Jessica flung herself out of bed. She was going to have to hurry to get ready in time to meet Sam.

She went to her dresser and started pulling out clothes. Violet socks. Deep purple leggings. Where was her big pink T-shirt? She tugged open another drawer and dumped half its contents on the floor. There were shirts in almost every shape and color imaginable—but no big pink top to wear with her purple leggings. Jessica snapped her fingers. There were definitely some advantages to having a twin sister, even one who wrote bizarre poetry. Elizabeth might not think as she did, but she was the same perfect size six. And she had almost the exact same pink top! Jessica would wear that and return it before Elizabeth knew it was gone.

Jessica was almost at her sister's dresser before she realized that Elizabeth was still in her room. Not only that, she was still in her bed. "What's the matter?" Jessica asked, concerned. "Are you sick?"

Elizabeth lay with her face to the wall. "No," she said in a flat, empty voice. "I just don't feel like getting up."

Elizabeth Wakefield, the girl for whom mornings were invented, didn't feel like getting up? Jessica went and stood over her. "Come on, Liz," she coaxed. "Don't let this plagiarism thing get you down. Just relax—it'll blow over in no time at all."

"No, it won't," Elizabeth mumbled. "Mr. Collins and everyone on *The Oracle* can't even manage to look me in the eye."

Jessica put her hand on her twin's shoulder.

"And Olivia—" Elizabeth's voice broke. "We've always been good friends, but now I feel like our friendship is ruined."

"That's *her* problem," Jessica said sharply. "It's because she knows she should support you in this but she can't deal with it. If you ask me, you should talk to her again. Olivia's a good person, Liz. I know you can make her listen."

"How can I make her listen if she rushes away in the opposite direction every time she sees me coming?"

Jessica looked down at the side of her sister's face, wondering how best to help her. "Well, you can't stay here all day," she said with a cheeriness she didn't feel. "Why don't you come to the race with me? Standing in mud all afternoon may not be the high point of your social life, but it beats lying in bed feeling sorry for yourself."

"Why don't you come shopping with me, Elizabeth?" Mrs. Wakefield asked. She was standing at the front door with her bag in her hand and a worried look on her face. "We could have lunch at that new café in the mall."

Elizabeth was sitting on the couch, pretending to read a magazine. She put on a cheerful face for her mother. "Thanks," she said lightly, "but I think I'd rather stay home today." She held up the magazine. "I have a lot of reading to catch up on."

Mrs. Wakefield didn't move. "I'm worried about you, sweetheart," she said gently. "This business with the paper . . ."

Elizabeth pushed a strand of hair out of her eyes. When she had told her parents what had happened with Mr. Collins, they had been as understanding as ever. Like Jessica, they thought the whole thing would resolve itself in no time at all. "You just hang in there," Mr. Wakefield had said. "The truth always comes out in the end." But the only truth Elizabeth felt sure of was that her life was ruined.

"I'm all right," Elizabeth said, hoping she sounded all right. "Really. I just want to be by myself." She picked up her magazine and began to read it intently.

As soon as the door closed behind her mother, Elizabeth threw the magazine down on the sofa. She wished Todd were coming over, but the doctor had said he still wasn't well enough to leave the house. "Two more days of juice and reruns," Todd had said. "I'm getting worried. I'm beginning to talk like Bugs Bunny."

Restless, Elizabeth went into the kitchen and fixed herself a cup of tea. She sat at the table, staring into her mug but not touching it. She left the tea on the table and went back to the living room. She sat down with her magazine again, but it was useless. She couldn't concentrate on hair-care tips and advice on healthy eating. *Jessica's right*, she told herself sternly. *You can't just mope around all day, feeling sorry for yourself.* Especially not when she had only herself to blame. If only she hadn't let herself get so behind on her essay . . . if only she hadn't accepted Rod's help . . . Elizabeth flopped back on the sofa. *If only it was two weeks ago. Then I'd do everything differently.*

Elizabeth was still lying on the couch when Enid called.

"How are you doing?" asked Enid. "You feeling any better yet?"

"Not exactly."

Enid's voice was sympathetic. "Well, I think I have some news that might cheer you up a little."

"Not unless you've discovered a way to send me back in time so I could avoid this whole mess."

"It's not quite that good," Enid answered. "But it's close. You know how Jessica's been going around being honest with everyone lately?"

Elizabeth groaned. "It's hard to ignore. She's driving us crazy with it. She almost started a fight between my mom and dad the other day, and the newspaper girl won't deliver the paper since Jessica told her she's not as good as the girl who had the route before."

Enid's laughter wrapped itself around Elizabeth like a familiar, comforting blanket. "Well, rest assured that you guys aren't the only ones Jessica's been driving crazy. You have no idea how many friends have stopped speaking to each other and how many couples have split up in the last week, all because Jessica decided to tell the truth."

As miserable as she was feeling, Elizabeth found herself caught up in Enid's story. "Jennifer Mitchell told me she was very angry with Jess for telling John Pfeifer that Jennifer was talking about breaking up with him before Jennifer could say anything to him."

"Almost everyone Jess knows is angry with her for something. Not only is she telling people exactly what she thinks of them, but if you ask her what someone else said about you, she'll tell you that, too." Enid paused. "But now Lila's come up with an idea for getting even."

"What's she going to do?" asked Elizabeth. "Have Jessica banned from the mall?"

Enid giggled. "Better. She's organizing a Total Honesty for Jessica Day!"

"A what?"

"A Total Honesty for Jessica Day! Everyone's going to tell Jessica the truth for one whole day. We'll see how much she likes her own medicine."

"That should be very interesting," Elizabeth answered. She knew exactly how much Jessica liked her own medicine, even in small doses.

"You have to hand it to Lila," Enid continued. "She may not be the nicest person in Sweet Valley, but she's a great schemer."

In spite of herself, Elizabeth found herself laughing. "Probably not as great as my sister," she said proudly. "Jessica's the best."

Although Olivia fell asleep trying to concentrate on Rod, it was Elizabeth she dreamed about. In her dream, Olivia was the new editor-in-chief of *The Oracle*. She was sitting in the office, conducting a staff meeting. Rod was there and so was Mr.

Collins. Rod and Mr. Collins were holding up a banner that had "Olivia Forever" written across it in large black letters. Outside it was snowing. It never snowed in southern California, but it had seemed normal in her dream. It had seemed normal, too, that Elizabeth was standing outside the half-open window, peering in. No one paid any attention to her. Warm and safe, Olivia and the others laughed and chatted as Elizabeth kept knocking on the window. "Why are you treating me like this?" she asked over and over. "You know I didn't mean it. I've always done my best. I've always stood by all of you." Every time Elizabeth spoke, Rod and Mr. Collins waved their banner. The others all pretended that they didn't hear. "Olivia!" Elizabeth called. "Olivia! Aren't you going to help me? Can't you see it's not fair?" Olivia walked over to where Elizabeth stood looking in, covered with snow. "I can't help you," Olivia said. "I'd like to, Elizabeth, but I really can't." She slammed the window shut—and woke up.

Olivia was still thinking about her dream when she sat down to breakfast. The memory of Elizabeth's bewildered face peering into the office made her shudder. *Put it out of your mind*, she ordered herself. *There's no use worrying about it.*

Intending to get her thoughts off Elizabeth, Olivia picked up the Saturday paper and turned to the weekend arts supplement. For a few seconds she just sat there, staring at the front page as though it were written in another language. There, in a box right in the center of the page, were the words "Poem in Motion," and underneath them

132

the name Olivia Davidson. "I don't believe this!" she said at last. "I just don't believe this!"

Mrs. Davidson looked up from the sports section. "What is it, Olivia? Is something wrong?"

"Wrong?" Olivia started laughing. "No, nothing's wrong." She jumped to her feet. "Mom, look at this! It's one of my poems! They've printed one of my poems on the front page of the arts supplement!"

But as Olivia leaned over her mother's shoulder to point out her poem, she had a thought that made her freeze. The person Olivia had to thank for her poem being printed was Elizabeth Wakefield. Elizabeth had encouraged her to send it in. Elizabeth had reminded her that poetry was important. Everything that Elizabeth had said in Olivia's dream was true. She had always been supportive. Olivia straightened up, only half listening to her mother's praise.

All through Saturday's race, Jessica stared into the distance and thought about her sister and Olivia. Something had to be done, and it didn't look as though Elizabeth herself was going to do it. Jessica frowned. She was always being asked to promise not to meddle in other people's lives, but this was different. Anything that affected her twin so deeply affected her as well. What sort of sister would she be if she stood by and watched Elizabeth be destroyed by something like this?

Jessica wasn't sure how long she stood there, the wheels of her clever mind turning and turning, but all of a sudden she was aware that Sam was coming toward her, his helmet swinging and a triumphant grin on his handsome face. He waved. Jessica waved back. *Yes*, she decided in that instant. *Honesty should begin at home.*

Every Saturday after a race, Sam rode his bike back to his house and Jessica drove his car. Then they would do something together for the rest of the afternoon.

"So what do you think, Jess?" Sam asked as they walked to the parking lot. "Where do you want to go after we drop off the bike?"

"To Olivia's," Jessica answered at once.

Sam looked baffled. "Why? Is she having a party or something?"

"Not unless it's a surprise party," Jessica said grimly.

Sam glanced over at her. "Let me guess," he said with an affectionate smile. "You're planning to interfere in your sister's life again."

"It isn't interference," Jessica said confidently. "It's honesty in action."

"Elizabeth!" Olivia exclaimed when she opened the door. "I was just—"

Jessica strode past her without waiting to be invited in. "Wrong twin," she said.

Olivia blinked in surprise. She had been thinking so much about Elizabeth since she saw her poem in the paper that she'd just assumed it was her. "Oh . . . uh, Jessica," she said, not bothering to try to hide her confusion. "Is there something I can do for you?" she asked.

Jessica flicked her hair over her shoulders and

folded her arms across her chest. "Yes, actually there is," she said coolly.

Olivia had never seen this stern, determined side of Jessica, and it surprised her as much as the fact that Jessica had dropped by at all.

"I came over because I wanted to talk to you about truth."

"Truth?" Olivia had heard that Jessica was on an honesty campaign, but she hadn't expected Jessica to try it on her.

"Yes," Jessica said. She took a deep breath and looked Olivia squarely in the eyes. "Elizabeth went to you with the truth because you were her friend and she needed your help. But instead of listening, you turned your back on her."

Elizabeth. All of a sudden, no matter where Olivia looked, there she was. In her dreams. At the breakfast table. In her living room. "Jessica, before you start—" Olivia began.

"Look, I know you're not responsible for anything that's happened, Olivia," Jessica said, talking right over her words, "but you're the one person who could do something to straighten things out because you're the person closest to Rod."

At the mention of Rod, a chill went through Olivia's heart. She thought back to the night before. It was as though she and Rod had agreed to pretend that Elizabeth didn't exist. As though by ignoring what had happened, what Elizabeth was going through, they could change the truth. "But Jessica, I don't—"

"I know," Jessica said impatiently. "You don't want to hear about it. But can't you see how ridiculous this whole situation is? Elizabeth's so upset she won't even come out of her room. Everything she's worked so hard for has been taken away, and why? Because things got out of hand."

"I'm sure that Rod never intended—"

"I don't know what Rod intended," Jessica cut in. "That's not what's important now. What's important is that he won't admit that he made a mistake. That's all he has to do, Olivia. Admit that he made a mistake."

Olivia stood in the center of her living room, looking into Jessica's eyes. *And all I have to do is admit that I've made a mistake, too,* she thought as she mechanically followed Jessica to the door.

Olivia watched Jessica stomp down the path, knowing she was right. It was time to stop deceiving herself. All of a sudden, everything was falling into place. Maybe Rod wouldn't admit it, but she knew she was right when she thought that he was interested in Elizabeth. She had been right to be suspicious when Rod suddenly produced that piece for *The Oracle.* She had been right to be upset when she saw him holding Elizabeth's hand. And when Elizabeth had said that the plagiarized material had come from Rod, she should have done something to help set the record straight.

Olivia sighed. It was time to force Rod to face the truth, too. No more excuses.

Ten

Olivia spent the rest of Saturday in her room, trying to work out her next move. Now that she had decided to face facts, she knew she had to investigate something that had been bothering her all along—Rod's article, his front-page feature story for *The Oracle*.

She had thought that what was bothering her was the fact that Rod had gone so far out of his way for Elizabeth, but in truth it was more than that.

After some searching she found the issue she was looking for at the bottom of the basket on her desk. It really was amazing, Rod writing a feature article overnight. It usually took him weeks to write a short essay, and even then Olivia often contributed by helping him make an outline before he started. She sat back on her bed and began to read it carefully.

She read the piece once and then read it again. The more she thought about it, the more she couldn't shake the feeling that there was something disturbingly familiar about it. She read it through a third time. Yes, there was definitely something very familiar about Rod's article. Olivia closed her eyes and tried to concentrate. There were phrases that seemed to echo through her head. *The responsibility of truth . . . the right of knowing . . .*

Olivia's eyes snapped open suddenly. "I don't believe this!" she said out loud. She reread the article one more time, then jumped up and began pulling books from the shelf. "It's in here somewhere, I know it is," she mumbled to herself as she began flicking through each volume.

The sun was fading from the sky by the time Olivia finally let out a deep breath and leaned back in her chair. She had discovered why Rod's article struck her as so familiar: at least three paragraphs of it hadn't been written by Rod at all. One had been written by Thomas Jefferson; one had been written by Thomas Paine; and one had been written by Benjamin Franklin. A short time ago, Olivia had helped Rod with a history essay in which he quoted from all three. She looked down at the textbooks that lay open before her. She had highlighted the paragraphs herself; Rod had lifted them from his history paper and put them into his piece for *The Oracle*, changing them only enough so they sounded contemporary. She stared at Rod's byline on the front page of the newspaper. "I'm really sorry about this, Rod," she said out loud. "But

Jessica's right. It's time for the truth to be heard. And if you won't do it, I'll have to do it for you."

She picked up the telephone and dialed Penny Ayala's number.

It wasn't until Sunday evening that Olivia finally got through to Penny, only minutes after Penny returned from the airport.

"Hi," Penny said brightly. "What's up, Liv? Tina said you'd been calling since yesterday. Did I miss the scoop of the century while I was in D.C.?"

Olivia laughed. "That's not as wild a guess as you might think," she replied. As succinctly and carefully as she could, she told Penny what had been going on in her absence. "I really don't know why Rod did it," she concluded. "I'm sure he started out innocently enough, and then it just sort of snowballed on him. But I feel awful about the way I've behaved toward Elizabeth. I guess I was so hurt and jealous that neither of you asked me to help out with *The Oracle* that I just refused to see the truth."

Penny sighed. "I had no idea you felt like that, Olivia. The only reason Elizabeth and I didn't ask you was because we both know how busy you are."

Two weeks earlier, this information would have thrilled Olivia. Now it only made her cringe. "I've really made a mess out of things," she said.

"Do you want me to go with you to talk to Mr. Collins?" Penny asked. "I know it's our word against Rod's, but I'm sure Mr. Collins will listen."

"Actually, I don't think it *is* just our word against Rod's," Olivia said. She explained what she had found out about the feature Rod did for Elizabeth. "Why don't we just ask Mr. Collins to take a look at it? I'm sure he'll recognize the paragraphs Rod lifted. And even if he doesn't, he's bound to realize that they weren't written by Rod. Then we can take it from there."

"And I thought Washington was full of schemers!" Penny laughed. "Maybe you should give up art for politics, Olivia. You're obviously a natural."

Jessica had never been a big fan of Mondays, but this Monday was ten times worse than any she had ever known. *I don't get it*, she said to herself as she cautiously made her way to her third class. *What's wrong with everyone today?* It was almost like one of those dreams where she went to school as usual, only to discover as she walked onto the stage in the auditorium that she was still wearing her pajamas. She looked around nervously. For some reason, everyone was on her case that day. She was sure she wasn't still wearing her pajamas, but the way people were treating her she might as well have been wearing a Kick Me sign.

It had begun in the girls' bathroom, before classes started. Jessica had been standing at the mirror, combing her hair and listening to the conversation around her, when Bruce Patman's name happened to come up. One of the girls had said that she couldn't understand why anyone would go out with Bruce Patman because he was so conceited. "You'd have to be out of your mind," Jessica had put in. But no sooner had the words left Jessica's mouth than Lila had materialized behind her. "Well, *you* must have been out of your mind, then," she had said. "Because if I remember correctly, not only were you crazy about Bruce, you went out with him yourself."

In math class Jessica had been telling the very cute mathematical genius who sat next to her how interested she had always been in algebra when Amy had suddenly leaned over and said in a loud voice, "No you aren't, Jessica! You told me you hate algebra, that you'd rather pierce your nose than do algebra." Then Amy had given her one of her biggest and phoniest smiles.

Jessica turned warily down the hallway. Every time she opened her mouth, someone popped up to jam her foot in it. All she had to do was just nod at someone, and the next thing she knew, they were telling her something she didn't want to hear. A few minutes earlier she had cheerfully greeted Maria Santelli, and Maria had replied with, "Is that a pimple you're getting on your chin, Jessica?" Then she had said a pleasant good morning to April Dawson, and April had come back with, "Have you put on a little weight, Jessica, or is it just that outfit you're wearing?"

Happy to have reached the classroom without further insults, Jessica slid into her chair. Robin Wilson leaned over to her with a concerned expression on her face. "Jessica," she whispered, "have I told you what I really think of your new cheer?"

Jessica made a face. "No," she said. "But I'm sure you will."

*   *   *

Penny and Olivia went to see Mr. Collins before school started. He was in the *Oracle* office, going through Jennifer's article for the upcoming issue. "Penny! Olivia!" He got to his feet with a smile. "What can I do for you?"

Olivia handed Mr. Collins the issue of the paper with Rod's article in it. "We just wondered if you'd had a chance to read this," she said.

Looking puzzled, Mr. Collins took the paper from her hand. "This is the issue that came out when I was home with the flu, isn't it?" He shook his head. "No, I never did read it, to be honest. Things have been so hectic since I got back . . ."

"Do you think you could just take a look at Rod's piece?" Penny asked.

Mr. Collins looked at them suspiciously. "Now?"

Olivia nodded. "If you could. It won't take long."

Mr. Collins wasn't even halfway through the article before a bewildered expression came over his face. He shifted in his chair and started at the beginning again. When he had read the piece through, without a word to Penny or Olivia, he read it once more. At last he looked up, throwing the paper onto the desk. "Just what is this?" he asked, looking from one girl to the other. "If I'm not mistaken, part of this article was written by Thomas Jefferson!"

"And Thomas Paine," said Penny.

"And Ben Franklin," added Olivia.

Mr. Collins leaned back. "I hope one of you is planning to tell me what's going on," he said.

Olivia cleared her throat, suddenly nervous.

"Go ahead," Penny urged her in a whisper.

"I don't know about this," Elizabeth said nervously. She looked from Todd to Enid. "Why do you think Mr. Collins wants to see me?"

Todd put his arm around her. "Maybe he's realized that he's made a mistake."

Enid nodded. "Yeah. Maybe Rod explained what happened."

Elizabeth looked down at her hands. "It's probably because Penny's back," she decided. "He probably wants to talk with her about what happened."

Todd and Enid each put a hand on her shoulder. "Well, there's only one way to find out," Todd said, and they gave her a gentle shove.

Elizabeth's heart was pounding so hard as she neared the *Oracle* office that she was sure people passing her could hear it. She could understand that Mr. Collins would want to discuss her suspension with Penny, but she wished that she didn't have to be present for it herself. She wasn't sure how much more humiliation she could stand.

She stopped at the office door, taking deep breaths to calm herself down. Much to her surprise, she suddenly became aware that there was someone right behind her. Turning quickly, she found herself staring into Rod Sullivan's dark brown eyes.

Rod flushed with embarrassment. "Elizabeth," he mumbled awkwardly. "What are you doing here?"

Somehow, she made her voice sound almost normal. "Mr. Collins asked to see me," she said.

Elizabeth could see Rod's expression change. All at once he looked more than embarrassed. He looked worried as well.

Just then Mr. Collins opened the door. "Elizabeth, Rod," he said, "come on in. I've been waiting for you."

Mr. Collins sat down behind his desk and picked up a copy of *The Oracle*. "I've just been sitting here catching up on some of the reading I missed while I was down with the flu. I came across the piece you did, Rod." He looked up. "It's certainly very nicely done. Very nicely done. Quite a step up from the work you usually do in class. Especially this bit here," he said. He began to read excerpts of Rod's article out loud. When he was done, he laid the paper back on the desk.

Elizabeth couldn't figure out what was going on. She stared at Mr. Collins in puzzlement.

Mr. Collins sat up straighter. "What about it, Rod?" he asked, his voice suddenly very serious. "Would you like to tell us where you got the inspiration for this piece?"

Elizabeth looked over at Rod. All of the color had drained from his face. "I . . . I don't know what you're talking about, Mr. Collins," he said. "Elizabeth asked me to—"

Mr. Collins cut him off. "We're not discussing Elizabeth at the moment," he said solemnly. "We're discussing you. How did you, an average English student at best, manage to do such an excellent job? The ideas here and the way they are expressed are absolutely first-rate."

"Well, I guess it's like you said. I guess I was inspired," Rod said quietly.

Mr. Collins got to his feet and came around to the front of the desk. "You're a plagiarist," he said flatly. "Not only are you a plagiarist, but you're not even a very clever one. You could at least have moved Thomas Jefferson's words around a little more, Rod. Made them a little more difficult to recognize."

"What?" Elizabeth gasped.

Mr. Collins said nothing, his eyes on Rod.

Rod looked down and stood in silence for several moments. "I don't have to stand here and listen to this," he said finally.

Mr. Collins pointed to the door. "You're right," he said. "You don't. You can leave and not come back."

Rod stopped in the doorway. "You're making a mistake, you know. I was only trying to help."

"Just don't make the mistake of lifting other people's words in the future," Mr. Collins advised him. "Because I'm going to be checking your English papers like a hawk from now on."

After Rod slammed the door behind him, Mr. Collins turned to Elizabeth. "Needless to say, I've figured out some explanation for your essay. I want you to know that it was wrong to use Rod's ideas the way you did."

Elizabeth felt tears well up in her eyes. "I realize that," she said softly.

"Yet at the same time, it is certainly not justified to accuse you of plagiarism. I encourage my students to discuss assignments among themselves and don't expect them to footnote one another." He paused. "I've decided I'm going to give you the opportunity to rewrite that paper."

"But . . . but I don't understand," she stammered. "How did you find out? Who told you?"

"Olivia," Mr. Collins said. "She figured out what Rod had done in the feature he wrote for you and used it to corroborate what you'd told her." His face softened. "I really wish you'd explained to me exactly what happened. It would have been so much easier."

Feeling weak with relief, Elizabeth collapsed in the nearest chair. "But I couldn't, Mr. Collins. I couldn't tell on Rod, especially not when I realized that I was guilty, too."

"Well, here's an idea, then," Mr. Collins said. "Why don't you write about plagiarism for your first feature, now that you're back on the staff of *The Oracle?*"

Elizabeth stared at him, speechless.

"You *are* back on the staff, aren't you?" he asked worriedly. "Penny will never forgive me if you won't come back."

"Oh, Mr. Colllins!" Elizabeth said. "I can't thank you enough. I—thank you so much!"

Mr. Collins smiled. "Don't thank me," he said. "Thank your friend Olivia."

Olivia had resolved that from then on she was going to be as honest with herself and with everyone else as she possibly could. For that reason, she was waiting outside of the *Oracle* office when Rod came out.

"Rod," she said gently, "we have to talk."

For a second she thought he was going to pretend that he didn't understand what she meant, but then he slowly shook his head. "I guess I sort of made a mess of things, huh?" he asked with an attempt at a laugh.

Olivia nodded. "Yes, I guess so."

He shifted uncomfortably. "You had something to do with this, didn't you?"

The night before, Olivia had felt nothing but anger for Rod, but now she felt almost sorry for him. It wasn't that he was a bad person, she realized. It was just that he hadn't known when to be honest with himself. "I just don't understand how you could have let things go so far," she said. "Especially when you saw what it was doing to Elizabeth."

Rod sighed, his eyes on the floor. "I don't know, Olivia," he said in a strangled whisper. "I guess you were right when you said I wanted to impress Elizabeth. But I couldn't see it clearly myself. I just kept telling myself I wanted to be friends. That I was being a good friend." His laughter sounded hollow. "I know it sounds impossible, but I really convinced myself that I hadn't done anything wrong."

Olivia touched his arm. "I guess lying to ourselves is the worst kind of all," she said.

Olivia was racing down the hallway when she turned a corner and practically knocked Elizabeth off her feet.

"Elizabeth! I'm sorry! I'm so sorry!"

"It's all right." Elizabeth laughed. "I was looking for you anyway."

Olivia shook her head. "I didn't mean I'm sorry only for bumping into you," she said quickly. "I meant for—for everything. I just hope you can forgive me."

"According to Mr. Collins, I should be thanking you, not forgiving you," Elizabeth said.

Olivia shook her head again. "No," she said. "You should be trying to forgive me. It's nothing I shouldn't have done days ago. And anyway, if it hadn't been for Jessica, I would probably still be behaving like a complete jerk."

"Jessica?"

Olivia nodded, wincing at the memory of her confrontation with Elizabeth's twin. "Uh-huh. She came over Saturday afternoon and really let me have it." Olivia explained about her conversation with Jessica. "Your sister's a real champion of truth and justice," she said with a smile. "She's going to put Superman out of a job if she isn't careful."

Elizabeth laughed. "At least she can't fly. Then we'd really be in trouble!" She held out her hand. "Friends again?"

"And co-workers!" Olivia said.

Jessica sat at the end of the lunch table, pretending to be deeply involved in eating her sandwich. Beside her, Lila, Amy, Caroline, and Robin all talked and laughed. Jessica was beginning to smell a rat. It couldn't be a coincidence that every time she opened her mouth someone would shout out, "That's not what you used to say!" It couldn't be an accident that Lila had chosen that day to criticize her clothes and that Amy was suddenly remembering every stupid thing she had ever said or done. Jessica took a bite of her sandwich, trying to remember how many times you were supposed to chew your food. Someone she barely knew had come over to her before and told her that she was eating too fast.

Annie Whitman stopped beside her. "Jessica," she said in a friendly voice, "I was wondering if you knew what A.J. Morgan says about the way you—"

"That's enough!" Jessica shouted. She could tell when she was being set up—especially since there was a wave of giggles going around the table. She turned to Lila, who was convulsed with laughter. "This is all your idea, isn't it, Lila Fowler?" she asked accusingly. "You put everybody up to this, didn't you?"

"Who, *me*?" gasped Lila.

Jessica crossed her arms. "What is this, Be Mean to Jessica Day?" she demanded.

Lila pulled herself together. "No," she said, still smiling mischievously. "It's Total Honesty for Jessica Day. How do you like it?"

Jessica was about to explain exactly how she felt about it—totally honestly—when her twin came charging over.

"I just wanted to have a word with you," Elizabeth said in her older-sister voice, "about going over to Olivia's house behind my back—"

"No more!" Jessica begged. She put her hands to her ears. "I don't want to hear it," she said. "I promise I'll never tell the truth again, no matter how hard people try to drag it out of me!"

"What are you talking about?" Elizabeth asked. "I wanted to thank you for being so honest and direct. You practically saved my life."

Jessica looked at her sister warily. "You're not mad at me for telling the truth?"

"Of course I'm not." Elizabeth gave her a hug. "I'm completely and totally grateful."

"Well, I'm glad someone here can appreciate the value of honesty," Jessica said with a pointed look at Lila.

But Lila was staring across the cafeteria with a distracted look on her face, obviously a million miles away.

"Uh-oh," said Jessica with a smile at the others. "Could it be that John Pfeifer has just come into the room?"

Amy, Caroline, and Robin laughed.

Lila turned her attention back to her friends. "Oh, get off it, Jessica," she said icily. "I was just thinking about something, that's all."

"Yeah, I know," Jessica said, gesturing to the table where John Pfeifer was sitting and looking over at them. "And I know *who* it was, too. Don't think I haven't seen you two talking at your lockers every morning for the past few days."

A shrewd look came into Caroline's eyes. "I knew Jennifer and John had split up," she said, smiling at Lila. "But I didn't realize there was something brewing between you and him."

"There is nothing *brewing* between me and John

Pfeifer," Lila said firmly. "We're just friends, that's all."

"Would you be willing to take a lie detector test?" Jessica teased.

What's going on between Lila and John Pfeifer? Find out in Sweet Valley High #90, DON'T GO HOME WITH JOHN.

The most exciting stories ever in Sweet Valley history...

FRANCINE PASCAL'S

SWEET VALLEY Saga

☐ **THE WAKEFIELDS OF SWEET VALLEY**
Sweet Valley Saga #1
$3.99/$4.99 in Canada   29278-1
Following the lives, loves and adventures of five
generations of young women who were Elizabeth and
Jessica's ancestors, The Wakefields of Sweet Valley
begins in 1860 when Alice Larson, a 16-year-old
Swedish girl, sails to America.

☐ **THE WAKEFIELD LEGACY: The Untold Story**
Sweet Valley Saga #2
$3.99/$4.99 In Canada   29794-5
Chronicling the lives of Jessica and Elizabeth's
father's ancestors, The Wakefield Legacy begins with
Lord Theodore who crosses the Atlantic and falls in
love with Alice Larson.

SWEET VALLEY HIGH

Celebrate the Seasons
with SWEET VALLEY HIGH
Super Editions

You've been a SWEET VALLEY HIGH fan all along—hanging out with Jessica and Elizabeth and their friends at Sweet Valley High. And now the SWEET VALLEY HIGH *Super Editions* give you more of what you like best—more romance—more excitement—more real-life adventure! Whether you're bicycling up the California Coast in PERFECT SUMMER, dancing at the Sweet Valley Christmas Ball in SPECIAL CHRISTMAS, touring the South of France in SPRING BREAK, catching the rays in a MALIBU SUMMER, or skiing the snowy slopes in WINTER CARNIVAL—you know you're exactly where you want to be—with the gang from SWEET VALLEY HIGH.

SWEET VALLEY HIGH SUPER EDITIONS

- ☐ **PERFECT SUMMER**
  25072-8/$3.50
- ☐ **SPRING BREAK**
  25537-1/$3.50
- ☐ **SPECIAL CHRISTMAS**
  25377-8/$3.50
- ☐ **MALIBU SUMMER**
  26050-2/$3.50
- ☐ **WINTER CARNIVAL**
  26159-2/$2.95
- ☐ **SPRING FEVER**
  26420-6/$3.50

☐ 27650-6	AGAINST THE ODDS #51	$2.95
☐ 27720-0	WHITE LIES #52	$2.95
☐ 27771-5	SECOND CHANCE #53	$2.95
☐ 27856-8	TWO BOY WEEKEND #54	$2.99
☐ 27915-7	PERFECT SHOT #55	$2.95
☐ 27970-X	LOST AT SEA #56	$3.25
☐ 28079-1	TEACHER CRUSH #57	$2.95
☐ 28156-9	BROKENHEARTED #58	$2.95
☐ 28193-3	IN LOVE AGAIN #59	$2.99
☐ 28264-6	THAT FATAL NIGHT #60	$3.25
☐ 28317-0	BOY TROUBLE #61	$2.95
☐ 28352-9	WHO'S WHO #62	$2.99
☐ 28385-5	THE NEW ELIZABETH #63	$2.99
☐ 28487-8	THE GHOST OF TRICIA MARTIN #64	$2.99
☐ 28518-1	TROUBLE AT HOME #65	$2.99
☐ 28555-6	WHO'S TO BLAME #66	$3.25
☐ 28611-0	THE PARENT PLOT #67	$2.99
☐ 28618-8	THE LOVE BET #68	$3.25
☐ 28636-6	FRIEND AGAINST FRIEND #69	$2.99
☐ 28767-2	MS. QUARTERBACK #70	$3.25
☐ 28796-6	STARRING JESSICA! #71	$2.99
☐ 28841-5	ROCK STAR'S GIRL #72	$3.25
☐ 28863-6	REGINA'S LEGACY #73	$3.25